TORNN'S MATE

A Dark Sci-Fi Alien Romance

Worldship Brides
Book 1

SUE LYNDON

Chapter 1

ELLIE

WILD SHIVERS RACK MY BODY. THOUGH THE DOCKING bay of the worldship is freezing, I'm shaking more from panic than the lack of warmth. As the minutes pass, the pervasive sense of dread sinks deeper into my bones, an agonizing chill that won't abate. For a fleeting moment, I worry I might go into shock.

Focus, I tell myself. *Be calm*. I swallow past the dryness in my throat and stare at the outer airlock door, studying every little detail in hopes of distracting myself. Eventually, my gaze drifts to a small circular window that allows a glimpse of the stars.

But I'm used to the large viewscreen in my family's lavish quarters, and while the docking bay is a cavernous area, I can't help but feel suffocated and on edge.

Need to get out of here.

Need to run.

I force in a deep breath and exhale slowly, watching as tiny white puffs escape my mouth. Fear churns in my gut, and my hands tremble harder at my sides. I can't run. There's nowhere to hide. No changing what's about to happen.

A shudder jolts the ship, and the lights flicker. Another reminder of our bleak situation. Another reminder that I have no choice.

The *Jansonna*, the worldship that houses the last of humankind, is nearly out of fuel. We're also in dire need of repairs. The five lowest decks are currently uninhabitable due to an uncontained gas leak, the water filtration system keeps breaking down, and environmental controls are in a constant state of malfunction.

With the temperature often below freezing, and the lack of clean water and nutritious food, people are getting scared and desperate. Our once peaceful ship has become plagued with violence, and it's not uncommon to hear blaster fire echoing down the corridors as security officers subdue pockets of unrest.

A door zips open and Captain Warren—my uncle —strides into the docking bay wearing a tense expression. As he joins the security officers standing near the airlock, his critical gaze sweeps over me and the other young women who are gathered.

There are thirty of us in total.

Thirty fertile women between the ages of nineteen and twenty-five.

Payment. That's what we are.

We're about to be handed over to the Darrvasons, a race of powerful but mysterious aliens, in exchange for fuel, supplies, and assistance in reaching a habitable planet. The Darrvasons are low on females. They need us for breeding purposes.

Will I ever see my mother again? My sister?

What about my fiancé, Nathan? He's a security officer and he promised to see me off, but he's not here. I don't think he's coming. His absence stings, but maybe it's for the best. We never officially broke up, but there's no way we're getting married now. Not when I'm about to leave forever. Not when I'm about to become the bride of a Darrvason male.

Tears burn in my eyes when I recall how several of my students had sweetly hugged me good-bye yesterday after class. After I'd delivered my final lecture, they'd gathered around me and wished me an emotional farewell. God, it had nearly broken me.

I blink rapidly against the burn in my eyes because the last fucking thing I need is for my uncle to catch me crying. Just this morning, he'd warned me to behave and set a good example for the other women, threatening to reduce my mother and sister's rations if I caused any trouble. He'd also threatened to withhold medical care, kick them out of their quarters, and force them to live in a cramped lower deck multi-family room.

You'll act sweet, grateful, and obedient as you stand in the docking bay waiting for the aliens to arrive. Keep your expression pleasant, eager, and devoid of fear.

His orders hadn't stopped there, and coldness grips me as the rest of his words resurface in my memory.

Whatever your Darrvason husband asks of you, you must comply with his wishes at once. No resistance whatsoever, no matter how barbaric you might find his behavior in the bedroom. You're among the first wave of human females the aliens are receiving from us, and I won't have the alliance fall apart because you decide to balk at being rutted and bred like an animal.

He'd grinned evilly after that, seeming to enjoy my shock.

I glance at the other women. None of us dare to speak, and most appear terrified. We're all wearing low-cut, form-fitting dresses created with shimmering fabrics. Our hair has been professionally styled, though none of us are wearing makeup. I suspect the command team doesn't want to be accused of false advertising when it comes to our looks, even though it's obvious they're trying to play up our appearance as much as possible.

I study the line of women, peering from face to face. The command team insists our names were chosen at random by a computer, but that's a filthy fucking lie if ever I heard one.

From what I can tell, the *chosen ones* can be divided into two groups. Group one: Those who have spent time in the brig for various infractions over the years, making them expendable in the eyes of the command team. Group two: The daughters and sisters of crew members who have spoken out or conspired against my uncle or his advisors.

I don't fit into either group, but I suspect I'm part of Captain Warren's unofficial public relations campaign. That is, I'm here to help garner sympathy and respect for my uncle, whose leadership abilities have come under increasing scrutiny as of late.

Look at the poor captain who had to sacrifice one of his nieces to the alien brutes.

Her name was picked at random, and he didn't overturn the results! He could've asked the computer for another name, but he didn't. He didn't abuse his power in that way.

Surely he cares about us, and surely he's doing everything he possibly can to save our ship and the last of humankind.

Yeah, I've heard the whispers. That's what people are saying, and it makes me want to puke. He doesn't care about me, and he won't miss me. The only person he cares about is himself. He's using me to prevent an all-out mutiny.

The aliens are due to arrive at any moment, and as the seconds tick by, the knot in my stomach tightens. I haven't personally glimpsed a Darrvason, but I've heard they are intimidatingly massive beings.

There's an abrupt shudder, and something blocks the small window near the airlock. My pulse quickens. It's the aliens. They're here.

For the briefest instant, I consider praying. But what good would it do? No one answered my prayers when my father was sick. He still died, and he suffered greatly along the way.

Please watch over your sister and mother, he'd gasped with his dying breath, *and don't trust the captain.*

Despair sinks its talons into me, and my spirits

plunge so low, it's a struggle to draw in my next breath. As I'd clasped my father's cold hand, I'd promised to always watch over them, but now I'm breaking that promise. Because I'm leaving.

There's another shudder, and suddenly the airlock opens. My uncle and his entourage move in front of the airlock, blocking my vision.

"This can't fucking be happening," the young woman standing next to me mutters.

I glance over and give her a sympathetic look. Thalia. That's her name. Her father was recently involved in a plot to overthrow my uncle. He was sentenced to death, along with several others.

"I'm sorry," I whisper. I'm not just apologizing for the fact that she's about to be bred by a fearsome alien creature, but for the recent loss of her father.

She draws in a long breath, but before she can reply, heavy footsteps echo in the docking bay, drawing our attention.

The security officers part to make way for our guests, and I watch in stunned disbelief as five impossibly huge beings emerge from the crowd. The dark-skinned aliens stand two heads taller than most of the human men. All wear tight black pants and long-sleeved shirts that appear molded to their muscular bodies.

"Oh my God," I whisper, then press my lips tightly together when my uncle shoots me an enraged look. He's standing so far away I doubt he heard me, though he must've seen my lips move. *Fuck.* I straighten and try not to look afraid. I try to look brave and set the example he wants me to set. *Sweet, grateful, and obedient.* I'll do anything to guarantee the safety of my mother and sister.

The tallest of the Darrvasons steps forward and inspects the line of young women. His eyes are dark purple, and I can't be sure, but it looks as though there's a red glow coming from underneath his shirt. Not all over, just along the neckline. But my focus quickly returns to those cold, assessing eyes of his.

It takes all my strength not to cringe or yelp when he settles his dark purple gaze on me. His nostrils flare and he takes two long steps forward. I gulp.

Why is he looking at me?

Captain Warren appears at the scary alien's side and clears his throat. "If you find any of these females lacking in any way, Admiral Tornn, we would be happy to provide you with an alternate."

Admiral? Holy shit. I've caught the freaking admiral's notice. I lower my head and concentrate on a scuff mark on the floor, wishing I could will myself invisible.

Admiral Tornn doesn't offer a reply. My flesh prickles with goosebumps, and my heart hammers faster in my chest. I don't have to look up to know he's still staring at me. His gaze is heavy, almost like a physical caress.

"All the females have promised to be cooperative, however, if any of them prove disobedient, you may return them for—"

"An alternate?" Admiral Tornn asks in perfect Galactic Common, speaking for the first time. His deep voice resonates in the vast space, bouncing off the walls and the ceiling. It also stirs something low in my belly, a strange but exciting sensation I've never experienced before.

"Yes," Captain Warren says with an eager nod. "An alternate."

"Alternates won't be necessary," the admiral replies. "If any of the human females are disobedient or prove uncooperative, they will be swiftly punished and forced to conform to the Darrvason way of life."

Swiftly punished? Forced to conform?

I suppress a shiver, and I notice Thalia moving closer to me, as though I might offer her some small measure of protection. I wish. I wish I could save all these women from the fate that awaits them. But without the alliance, the *Jansonna* likely won't last another moon cycle before environmental controls completely give out. I don't like the decision my uncle made, and I'm both hurt and furious he selected my name, but I understand how serious our situation has become. I understand the alliance is necessary.

Captain Warren starts to wax poetic about how beautiful, fertile, and well-mannered the thirty of us are. He also talks about how honored he is that the Darrvasons have chosen humankind for such an alliance. Normally, my uncle bows to no one. Nor does he try to impress anyone. The ridiculous, over-the-top way he's sucking up to the admiral is so pathetic, I find a smile tugging at my lips.

Shock fills me when one of the women farther

down the line snorts with amusement. No idea who made that noise, but I want to be her new best friend.

I glance up in time to see my uncle stiffening and shooting a murderous look at one of the thirty, a blonde who has bigger balls than me. Or maybe she has nothing left to lose. Maybe her family is gone and there isn't anyone left she needs to protect. I vaguely recognize her as one of the women who's spent time in the brig, though I can't recall her crimes.

"You and your men may leave the docking bay," Admiral Tornn says, interrupting my uncle. "Once the thirty females are secure in our custody aboard the *Haxxal*, I will send over a team to start making repairs on your ship."

Why does the admiral's voice keep vibrating through me, causing my core to clench? Why do I feel drawn to him? It's taking all my self-control not to glance up and study his purple gaze. To become lost in it.

I continue staring at the mark on the floor as I try to sort out my conflicting thoughts.

"Very well. The *Jansonna* will hold position and remain docked to the *Haxxal* as we await the arrival of your people," Captain Warren says, and I hear the scuffle of boots as the guards and the command team depart.

Finally, I look up, and my eyes instantly collide with the admiral's. My stomach lodges in my throat. Has he been staring at me this whole time? There's an intensity to his gaze that leaves me unsettled. He almost looks… angry.

Be brave, be brave, be brave.

I lift my chin a notch, forcing myself to hold his intimidating stare. To my surprise, a glint of amusement sparks in his eyes. It vanishes so quickly, however, that I wonder if I only imagined it.

He finally looks away from me, and all at once I can breathe again.

"I am Admiral Tornn," he says in a booming voice as he peers up and down the line of women, "and on behalf of Emperor Radakk, I would like to welcome you to the Darrvason Empire. You'll be selected by your new mate immediately upon boarding the *Haxxal*." He pauses and his eyes meet mine again, causing my breath to falter. "Let us depart."

I lower my gaze and scramble to pick up my suitcase. The five aliens move along the line of women, herding us closely toward the airlock. As if any of us would succeed in escaping. Pretty sure the door leading to the corridor is locked. My uncle would've made sure of that.

A tense silence hovers as we approach the airlock. We traverse a narrow but long docking tunnel that's lit with strange glowing symbols in various colors. I clutch my suitcase and experience a bout of dizziness when it hits me that I'm actually boarding an alien spacecraft. I've seen a variety of alien vessels over the years, but until now I've never set foot on one. There's a thump, and I turn in time to see the faint glow of the *Jansonna's* docking bay vanish, my last glimpse of home.

Admiral Tornn's proclamation from moments ago rings in my ears.

You'll be selected by your new mate immediately upon boarding the Haxxal.

I know nothing about Darrvason customs surrounding marriage or mating or whatever they want to call it. But I'm relieved we'll only belong to *one* male each, that we won't be expected to copulate with multiple Darrvason males.

Why are they low on females? I can't help but speculate on the reason. Did war or disease claim them? Did another race of aliens steal them?

Fear clutches my heart as I worry that whatever tragedy befell Darrvason females will occur all over again. Maybe we're not safe in their empire.

As I continue walking down the narrow passage-way, I feel as though I'm being led to my doom.

A shuddering breath escapes me. What sort of life awaits me among the aliens? Will my mate treat me as a broodmare and nothing more? Will I be allowed to raise the children I bear, or will they be taken away from me not long after birth?

My imagination runs wild with a thousand terrible scenarios.

Not for the first time today, I find myself blinking back tears.

I'm so afraid. I can pretend to be brave all I want, but there's no chasing away the deep fear that leaves me chilled to the bone.

The corridor opens to a docking bay that's vastly different from that of the *Jansonna's*. One entire wall looks like a giant window. Surely I'm not gazing at open space. It must be a window of sorts, and a very strong one at that. Otherwise, we'd be sucked outside to our deaths.

Astonished, I peer at the window only to realize it's not a window after all. It's a force field. A medium-sized vessel zips through the invisible barrier, causing the shield to shimmer for a brief instant—before coming to land with a faint thud. Whoa. Scientists aboard the *Jansonna* are just starting to experiment with force field technology, but I've never seen it in action before.

There are more huge, dark-skinned aliens in the docking bay. All are dressed in a similar fashion with black pants and tight long-sleeve shirts that accentuate their sculpted pectoral muscles. Their textured skin glimmers under the lights. Most possess purple eyes, though I spot a few with red gazes. Some have close cropped hair and smooth faces, while others sport longer tresses and beards.

Despite their immense size, they're humanoid enough, which is a huge relief. Two arms. Two legs. Six fingers on each hand. I don't see any weird appendages or tentacles or claws. During our journey through the stars, humankind has encountered its fair share of very *alien* aliens, including some who've wanted to eat us.

A hatch on the medium-sized vessel opens, and a huge Darrvason male steps out. He's flanked by a few other males. He strides in my direction, and my pulse accelerates when I fear he's set his sights on me, only for him to step around me and grasp Thalia.

"This one's mine," he says, and I get the sense that he's someone of importance among the Darrvasons. I mean, he's in the presence of the freaking admiral of the entire fleet and he's acting like the big bad boss man.

"She is yours, Emperor Radakk," Admiral Tornn says as he walks closer.

I exchange a worried look with poor Thalia. The emperor! Oh, wow. Oh, shit.

The emperor takes Thalia's suitcase and guides her out of the docking bay. She doesn't say a word, though I can sense her disbelief and fear. A wide door zips open upon their approach and then they're gone. I pray the emperor will treat her with kindness. But do the Darrvasons possess any decency at all?

Swiftly punished. Forced to conform.

That's what Admiral Tornn said would happen to those who prove troublesome. A sense of helplessness falls over me, and I feel a smidge guilty that I'm suddenly worried more for myself than I am for Thalia or the other women.

What if my mate hurts me? What if he's cruel?

Nathan's handsome face flashes in my mind. God, how I'll miss him. He's sweet and kind and everything I ever wanted in a husband. I could easily picture myself having children and sharing a happy life with him aboard the *Jansonna*.

The vision soon fades and is replaced with

Admiral Tornn, who has moved to stand directly in front of me.

He levels a disapproving look at me, as though he can sense I was just thinking about the human man I love.

His nostrils flare. He leans close and takes a deep inhale.

Instinctively, I step back. I can't help it. All the Darrvasons scare me, but he frightens me the most.

His commanding presence makes me tremble, and the sharpness of his gaze makes me feel stripped of all my defenses.

There's movement around us as other alien males in the docking bay come forward to claim their mates. How they decide who belongs to whom, I have no idea. Maybe they're picking the woman they find most attractive. It might be as simple as that.

"You're mine."

"I want you."

"Come with me, human female."

Though I hear other women being claimed and escorted out of the docking bay, I can't tear my gaze from Admiral Tornn.

I start to get a bad feeling.

As I peer up at him, my neck begins to ache. How tall is he, anyway? Seven feet? Seven and a half? His size intimidates me as much as his steely air of command and those cold purple eyes.

It's not until I realize we're completely alone in the docking bay that I start shaking so hard, I lose the grip on my suitcase. Before it can crash to the floor, the admiral's hand shoots down and he grasps the handle in a reflex so fast it's eerily unhuman.

My stomach flips as I wonder how quickly he can run. Not that I was thinking about escaping him at present, but if I ever needed to flee for my own safety? Damn. I would be so screwed.

He steps closer and places a finger beneath my chin, forcing me to hold his gaze. *He's touching me.* My dread intensifies.

And yet…

And yet I'm also filled with undulating warmth, and I have the strangest urge to lean into his touch, to step into his arms and breathe deeply of his rich, masculine scent.

We're alone. All the other women have been claimed.

I'm the only one left.

Oh God oh God oh God.

His next words are spoken in a deep, possessive tone.

"You are *mine*, human female."

Chapter 2

TORNN

SAVAGE HUNGER CONSUMES ME AS I TRAIL MY FINGERS over the female's soft cheek. I also touch her hair, tucking an errant strand behind her tiny, delicate ear. She's trembling and her breath occasionally catches in her throat, but she doesn't try to escape my attentions.

Shock and amazement flare from deep within my psyche. She's the first female I've touched since reaching adulthood, and a long, still moment passes during which I wonder if she is truly real. I tense, half-worried I will awake from a blissful dream.

My need for her is so overwhelming, I experience a sudden attack of dizziness as my dual shafts harden in my pants.

The instant our eyes had locked on the *Jansonna*, I'd known she was the woman for me. The female I would claim, the female who would bear my sons and daughters. It was a *knowing* that made my blood hum and my heart resonate with longing.

I tell myself it's pure animalistic need and nothing more. Our union will be one of convenience and necessity. I need a woman for breeding purposes, and her sacrifice will ensure her own people don't fade into the stars. I'll protect her and provide for her, and perhaps in time we might cultivate a friendship of sorts, but a deeper connection—a heartbond—well, it simply isn't possible.

Even so, I ache to get the little dark-haired beauty to my quarters and plant my seed in her womb. I ache to master her body and fully claim her as mine. Soon. Very soon.

Before we retire for the night, she will belong to me. Completely.

I grasp her upper arm and guide her out of the docking bay. When I notice her struggling to keep pace with my rapid strides, an unexpected pang of concern tightens in my chest, and I slow my steps.

As we head down the nearest corridor, a team of engineers passes us on their way to the human worldship. We exchange a brief greeting in Darrvason and I wish them good fortune, though I have no doubt they will succeed in overhauling the *Jansonna*.

Once repairs are complete, Captain Warren will provide us with one hundred more fertile human females, and once we successfully guide the human worldship to a habitable planet, we'll receive a final payment of two thousand fertile human females.

More than enough to turn the tide in our fight against extinction.

As we walk, I can't stop stealing glances at my bride. Her eyes are startlingly blue, and though her pale skin doesn't glimmer in the same way mine does in the overhead lights, I still find her immensely pleasing to behold.

"Will the other women be treated well?" she asks as we turn down the corridor that leads to my quarters.

Her question surprises me. "Of course they will be treated well. Why would we harm a female? We need women for companionship and procreation."

She shoots me an odd look that I can't quite read. "You mentioned punishment to my uncle and said we would be forced to conform."

Again, her words surprise me. "Your uncle? Captain Warren is your uncle?" I'm stunned that the captain would surrender a family member to my people. Wouldn't he want to see her safely settled on a planet with the rest of the human race? Wouldn't he miss her?

She swallows hard. "Yes, the captain is my uncle." She says it grudgingly and her blue eyes flash with malice, though I can't tell whether her displeasure is directed at me or her uncle. "Well? Exactly how will your males treat a human woman who's been disobedient? What will you do? Beat her? Toss her in the brig? I want to know what sort of punishment we'll face." She lifts her chin in challenge, and I promptly tighten my grip on her arm.

"We will finish this discussion in private," I say in a commanding tone. Security officers and maintenance workers occasionally pass us by, and I have no desire to get into an argument with my human female in front of others.

She tries to pull her arm from my grasp, but I don't release her. Her defiance is shocking. Darrvason females are typically timid and obedient, though it's not unheard of for one to require chastising on occasion.

My shafts thicken at the prospect of taming my little human mate. If she tests me, I won't hesitate to administer a swift and fitting punishment.

"Where are you taking me?"

"To my quarters. Now, no more talking. Not until we are alone."

I hurry her through the corridor to my abode. The door zips open and I lead her inside. After placing her luggage on the floor, I release her arm.

A whimper catches in her throat as she looks over her shoulder and watches the door zip shut. We're alone. Finally. Her chest starts rising and falling more rapidly, drawing my gaze to her bosom. The gown she's wearing leaves little to the imagination, though I still long to see her unclothed.

What color are her nipples?

What does the area between her thighs look like?

Eight days ago, I'd sent a team of physicians to the *Jansonna* to examine several human females—to verify that they would indeed be compatible with Darrvason males—but I wasn't able to accompany them, so I haven't yet glimpsed a naked human female with my own eyes. My male appendages throb as I envision stripping off my mate's gown, parting her thighs, and thrusting deep.

"Welcome to my quarters," I say. "This is where you will live while we are aboard the *Haxxal*." I don't bother to tell her it's where we'll both live for the foreseeable future. The humans aren't the only ones in search of a new planet to call home.

"Am I a prisoner here?" She draws in a shaky breath. "Or will I be permitted to freely roam your ship?" Her gaze darts to the massive viewscreen that nearly takes up an entire wall of my quarters. From here, we have a clear view of the *Haxxal's* docking tunnel as it slowly retracts from the *Jansonna* and folds back into the ship.

"You aren't a prisoner, however, you aren't yet free to leave my quarters and roam the ship."

"What do you mean?" Confusion flits across her face.

"You will not be permitted to leave my quarters until we have mated many, many times *and* I am certain I can trust you to behave properly."

Her face pinkens, her cheeks taking on a beautiful flush. "Why do we have to mate first… and why-why multiple times?"

"Because I want you thoroughly covered in my scent to ward off all other males. I will not risk another male taking interest in you and trying to claim you." I close the distance between us and cup her face in one hand, then trail my thumb across her cheek.

"You belong to me, and I would kill anyone who tries to take what's mine."

My gaze falls to her plump lips, and the urge to kiss her until we're both breathless assails me, yet I find myself holding back when her eyes glimmer with fear. Why am I holding back? She's *mine*.

"What is your name, human female?"

She steps away from me, but I follow her. I drop my hand from her face and pull her flush against my body. She gasps and wiggles in my hold, and the feel of her fighting activates my darker, more predatory urges.

I want to ravish her and conquer her.

I want to make her whimper and beg.

As though sensing I'm about to lose control, she freezes in my arms and peers up at me, her face still flushed, her eyes wide and pleading.

"Tell me your name." I delve a hand into her silken hair, tangling my fingers in her locks and giving a slight tug. She will soon learn that I don't like having to repeat myself.

"Ellie," she says. "My name is Ellie."

"Ellie," I repeat, and my two cocks pulse harder against her stomach. I know she can feel the evidence of my excitement. Part of me hopes she resumes her struggles. How I would love to subdue her, tear off her clothing, and rut her in the middle of the floor.

An intoxicating scent reaches my nose, and I inhale deeply of the aroma I suspect is her anticipation. According to the team who'd visited the *Jansonna*, human women become slick between their thighs when they are eager to be claimed, just as Darrvason females do.

My spirits lift, and my shafts thicken further. I ache to plunge inside Ellie and feel her inner walls contract around me.

"What are you doing?" She tries to wiggle out of my arms but ceases moving when her elbow pushes against my crotch, nudging one of my appendages. I nearly growl with the pleasure of it.

"I am smelling you, Ellie." I savor another long, drawn-out inhale, and this time, I can't suppress a growl. "The wetness that is growing between your thighs smells delicious. I can't wait to taste it."

She whimpers and shakes her head back and forth. "Please. I-I can't breathe. I need to sit down."

Concern for her flares inside me, and I promptly scoop her up in my arms and carry her to a large, plush sofa that overlooks the stars. From here, there's a clear view of the numerous vessels in my fleet, as well as the *Jansonna*, which will continue traveling with us until we deliver the humans to a habitable planet.

I set Ellie on the sofa and hurry to the kitchen for a cup of water. Once I return to her side, I press the cup into her hand and beckon her to drink.

She gives the beverage a wary look and sniffs it.

"It's just water," I assure her.

She takes a cautious sip and swallows. "Thank you," she murmurs.

"Are you unwell? I can summon a physician."

"No doctors. Please. I'm fine." She sucks in a long breath and slowly exhales. "I'm just nervous. Um, when exactly do you plan to claim me? Right now? Later today?"

I sit next to her and place a hand upon her thigh. I try not to frown when she flinches at my touch. But I don't remove my hand. She's my mate and I have every right to touch her, every right to kiss her and claim her.

I open my mouth, preparing to tell her that I intend to fill her with my hardness before the day is over, but that glimmer of fear from earlier returns to her eyes, causing me to falter. "I wish to claim you today, Ellie, however—"

The visitor bell suddenly echoes throughout my quarters, and I jump to my feet and glance at the door with a snarl.

Who would dare to interrupt me at a time like this?

"Excuse me," I say through clenched teeth. "I'll be right back."

I approach the door and give the individual on the other side a murderous look before I even realize who it is. Captain Varll.

"What is it?" I hiss in our native tongue. I enter the corridor and let the door shut behind us, not wanting Ellie to overhear our conversation. Even though she cannot speak Darrvason, she might be able to discern some meaning from our tone and gestures.

The captain clears his throat. "Forgive me for coming here, Admiral, but this is a sensitive matter, and I didn't want to send a message over the comm system and risk others hearing it. I don't wish to create a panic." He pauses for the briefest instant, the color draining from his face before he continues. "Security Officer Paddax has been attacked by his new human mate. She injected him with something—poison or a virus of some type, we aren't certain yet—and he's in critical condition, though the physicians claim they can save him. I thought you might want to know, Admiral. The offending female has been placed in the brig temporarily."

A growl rumbles from my throat. *Fluxx.*

How could this have happened?

"She used a hypospray?" I ask.

"Yes. She had it hidden between her thighs, Admiral."

"Contact all the males who left the docking bay with a human female," I say. "Apprise them of the situation and order them to frisk their females *thoroughly*. Also order them to search their female's luggage."

"Understood, Admiral." He spins on his heel and rushes down the corridor.

I don't return to my quarters immediately. I stand outside the door, trying to gather my thoughts and rein in my anger.

How could a female attack her mate? It's unthinkable.

I stare at the door, wondering if this was a coordinated attack. Do other human females plan to inject their males with the same harmful substance? Is Captain Warren involved?

Darkness gathers in my mind. Does Ellie have any

contraband in her possession? A small weapon, or a poison-filled hypospray?

I return to my quarters and settle a fierce look upon her. Her eyes widen as I approach the sofa where she's sitting. I crouch in front of her, holding her gaze.

She sets the water aside with a trembling hand. "Is-is something wrong, Admiral Tornn?"

Hearing my name escape her lips for the first time causes an unexpected warmth to flow through me. It catches me off guard, and I don't start interrogating her just yet. Instead, I study her expression for any hint of deceit while also admiring her beauty.

Is she waiting for the right moment to withdraw a weapon or a hypospray from her gown and try to end me?

Why would the humans want to harm us?

But the more I think about it, the more I realize Captain Warren and his command team likely aren't behind the attack on Paddax. It wouldn't make sense for the human leaders to want any of my people dead. Our weaponry is vastly superior to that of the humans. We could destroy the *Jansonna* with the press of a button.

In all likelihood, Paddax's mate had acted alone, and she probably wasn't under orders from Captain Warren. The very survival of the human race depends upon maintaining the Darrvason-human alliance. They need us.

"I'm afraid there's been an incident," I finally reply.

"What kind of incident?" She glances at the

viewscreen, her gaze on the *Jansonna*. "Is the human worldship okay? Please tell me there wasn't an accident on board. I-I know the ship is in terrible condition, but…" Her voice trails off and she wraps her arms around her body as her shaking increases. "My mother and sister live on the upper decks."

"Nothing happened aboard the *Jansonna*," I'm quick to assure her. "I'm certain your family is fine. I've sent a team of our most skilled engineers to start making repairs on the human worldship. We passed them in the corridor just outside the docking bay."

She places a hand to her chest and releases a quick breath. "*Oh*. Oh, thank goodness." She peers at me with questions brimming in her eyes. "Um, did something happen on the *Haxxal*, or on another Darrvason ship?"

"One of the thirty human females has attacked her mate, leaving him in critical condition. She injected him with something."

She gasps. "Will he live?"

"The doctors believe they can save him."

A relieved sigh escapes her, and her shoulders sag briefly. Then she straightens and grabs my arm, giving me a beseeching look. "Please have mercy. Please don't kill the woman, and please don't break your alliance with my people."

I place my hand atop hers, enjoying her touch despite the gravity of the situation. "I have no intention of killing the woman. She is currently in the brig, but she'll be returned to her mate once he recovers. In the meantime, she will not be mistreated. As for the alliance with your people, I wish to maintain it. I won't let the actions of one allow it to collapse."

Her eyes fill with relief. "Thank you, Admiral Tornn. Truly. Thank you." A somber look falls over her. "I'm glad the Darrvosan male will survive, and I'm sorry for what the woman has done. She did a terrible thing, I can't claim she didn't, but... what will happen once she's returned to her mate? Will he... *hurt her?*"

"It's possible he'll decide to punish her," I say, "but it's also possible he'll be forgiving. I don't know the male in question very well, so I cannot speak for him. If he does punish her, the worst she can expect is a whipping."

Ellie's eyes grow larger, but she doesn't immediately respond. I'd expected her to plead for more leniency on behalf of the woman, but she remains quiet and appears deep in thought. Troubled. Anxious.

"What would you do?" she asks in a whisper. "If I attacked you, what would you do?"

"Are you asking if I would punish you?"

There's a sudden charge in the air between us. She inhales a shaky breath, then nods. Her eyes remain wide, and I can see her pulse fluttering on her slender neck.

"That would depend entirely upon the circumstances. What motives led you to attack me, and whether you harbored any shame over your actions. If you were driven by true hatred, I doubt punishing you would help matters. In that case, I would probably attempt to earn your trust rather than give you a thrashing. But make no mistake—I would not be pleased by your betrayal."

I reach for her and slowly comb my fingers through her hair. She trembles under my attentions but doesn't try to escape. Her exotic features mesmerize me, especially the softness of her dark locks, the golden undertone of her skin, and the tiny brown flecks in her otherwise blue eyes.

"Well," she says after a long pause in conversation, "I have no plans to attack you or anyone else on this ship. I-I'm sad that I had to leave my family behind on the *Jansonna*, but I want the alliance to succeed. I would never do anything to jeopardize it. I promise."

She seems sincere, and I doubt she's in possession of any contraband, but I can't ignore what happened to Paddax. I rise to my feet and draw her to stand in front of me. She follows my lead as the worry in her eyes deepens, though she lifts her chin in a show of bravery, a habit of hers that I'm beginning to find endearing.

"Is it time?" she asks in a soft voice. "Time for us to… *mate*?"

At the mention of mating, my cocks swell larger and strain against the front of my pants. But we can't mate yet. What kind of admiral would I be if I didn't follow my own orders? I can't let my primal need to be inside her cloud my judgment.

"Before we mate, Ellie, there's something I must do."

"Oh? What's that?"

"To ensure that no other human females have brought weapons or hyposprays aboard the ship, I've ordered the males from the docking bay to frisk their mates thoroughly, as well as to search their luggage." I grasp her arm and pull her closer. "I expect your full cooperation in this, Ellie."

Chapter 3

ELLIE

He searches my suitcase first. I stand close by, watching as he riffles through my clothing and the few personal items I'd packed. I hold my breath as his large fingers curl around my tablet that contains thousands of books. It's a decades old piece of technology and my most precious possession. But to my great relief, he only peers at it for a second, then gingerly sets it aside. Next, he takes his time and carefully slides his fingers along every inch of the bag.

Once he's finished, he closes the suitcase and rises to his feet. He turns to face me and it's all I can do to keep from running.

He wants to frisk me, and he expects my full cooperation. If I fight him, will he punish me? I don't want to find out, so I resolve that I'll be as obedient as possible. I won't lie—I'm terrified by the prospect of a whipping.

Heat unfurls inside me as his gaze runs up and down my body. I try very hard not to glance at his crotch, but fail. Dammit. I'd noticed a massive bulge earlier, but it seems to have grown considerably in a few short minutes. Clearly, the prospect of putting his hands on me is inciting his desires.

But heated pulses keep affecting my core, and I can't seem to catch my breath. To my shock, I realize he's not the only one who's excited by the thought of him frisking me. The idea of his hands roaming over my body as he inspects me and searches for contraband is oddly titillating. Especially when I have no choice but to comply.

An unexpected wave of submission sweeps over me, as though I can't help but yield to his authority. My face grows warmer and the aching between my thighs intensifies.

"I think it will be easier to frisk you in the bedroom, Ellie." Before I can decide whether to protest, he's already guiding me away from the sitting area.

We enter a spacious room that's dominated by the largest bed I've ever seen. My thoughts race as I consider my predicament. I think of my mother and sister and everyone else on the *Jansonna* whom I care about. Nathan. Especially Nathan.

I swallow hard as my shaking increases. I must be the meek, obedient wife Tornn wants me to be. I must follow his commands and do everything in my power to help keep the alliance strong. I mean, it's not like I'm about to mate with some random officer aboard the *Haxxal*.

I'm about to mate with the goddamn admiral.

Even though Tornn claimed alternate females wouldn't be necessary—though it would seem even attempted murder isn't grounds for sending a woman back to the *Jansonna* in exchange for another—I still can't risk the fallout of misbehavior.

If Tornn were to make a passing comment to Captain Warren about my rebelliousness, my asshole of an uncle might very well follow through with his threats against my mother and sister.

I lower my head as I move to stand by the bed. Tornn releases my arm, but he remains so close that I can feel the waves of heat rolling off his huge, muscular body. He settles his hands on my hips, and a gasp lodges in my throat. He leans down and boldly sniffs the top of my head. I flush as a pleased rumble escapes him.

The desire rushing through my body is unfamiliar, and I don't know how to handle it. What to do with it. Aboard the *Jansonna*, everyone is given compulsory hormone suppression shots starting at an early age, which means very few humans experience the urge to physically copulate these days. Furthermore, reproduction is carefully planned and achieved in a fertility lab. It's all I know.

But I'm past due for my yearly shot. I should've gotten it one month ago, now that I think about it, but I was never called to the medical bay for a booster.

Humans encountered the Darrvasons just over a month ago. Only days later, my uncle informed me that I would be among the first wave of brides.

Awesome. I'm experiencing arousal for the first time in my life, and it happens to be in the presence of a huge, domineering alien who wants to breed me.

I try not to think about why I didn't feel the urge to jump Nathan's bones before my departure.

Tornn places a finger beneath my chin and tilts my head upward. My gaze collides with his and all the air whooshes from my lungs. His visage softens just a little, and I can't help but marvel at how handsome he is. He has a strong square jaw, a long straight nose, high cheekbones, and there's an otherworldly beauty to him that makes it difficult to look away.

"You're trembling, sweet human."

I suck in a steadying breath. "I'm sorry. I-I can't help it." My heart thunders in my chest. Is he displeased with me? I try to calm myself enough to stop shaking, but my deepening arousal converges with the healthy fear I have of Tornn, leaving me a quaking mess. At any moment, I'm certain my weakened legs will give out and I'll tumble to the floor.

"You don't need to apologize." He strokes my cheek. "Are you truly that frightened of me?"

My throat closes up, and I can only manage a quick nod. Of course I'm *that* frightened of him. He's so huge and powerful, he could do whatever he wanted to me, and I wouldn't be able to stop him. I'm utterly defenseless against him, and I've never felt more vulnerable in my life.

Swiftly punished. Forced to conform.

His threat keeps echoing in my head.

Would I ever displease him enough to warrant a punishment?

"Are there rules?" I suddenly blurt. "Specific rules that you expect me to follow? I don't want to accidentally break one."

His eyes light with amusement as he continues stroking my face and even plays with my hair. He's silent for so long, I start to think he won't answer, but finally he says, "I don't have a prepared list of rules for you, sweet human, *but* know that I expect you to be an obedient and well-mannered wife."

"That's not very helpful," I say, and instantly wish I could retract my words.

To my immense relief, he smiles. His eyes twinkle in a thousand shades of purple as a deep chuckle reverberates from his throat. But then I notice his white, *pointed* teeth. I can't look away. His teeth. Oh my God, his teeth...

He could rip my throat out if he wanted to.

"Do you not understand the definition of obedience?" he eventually asks, a smile still tugging at his mouth.

I flush hotly and press my lips together, fighting the urge to make a flippant comment. He's not the one who might receive a *whipping* if he makes a wrong move. I have every right to question him about rules, every right to fear the outcome of a misstep.

"It's simple, really, Ellie. If I issue a command, you

must follow it. I am your husband—your master—and my word is law."

"But physical punishment," I whisper, "forgive me, but that is so… barbaric." *Shut up shut up shut up.* Why can't I stay quiet? Why can't I nod meekly and let him get on with the frisking? I swallow hard as I await his response, praying I haven't angered him.

"Barbaric?" His smile fades.

He leans down and places his lips at my ear. His breath wafts along my neck, and a shiver rushes down my spine and somehow merges with the heated pulses in my core, the intense physical sensation nearly causing me to whimper.

"Perhaps after I finish frisking you, sweet human," he says in a deep, rumbling tone that further provokes my desires, "I will show you just how barbaric I can be." He takes a long inhale and growls. "The scent of your slickness is driving me mad with the need to be inside you, to pound into you with my cocks and fill you with my seed over and over again."

This time, a whimper does escape my throat.

Cocks. He said *cocksss.*

Plural.

Holy freaking hell. No wonder his bulge is so huge.

My legs tremble harder, and I start to feel lightheaded.

Yet my excitement doesn't abate. The quaking pulses between my thighs keep coming, faster and harder, and I swear the wetness in my panties keeps growing. Arousal. Actual arousal. He's right. I am getting slick. Embarrassingly so. I wish he couldn't smell it. I wish I could hide my desires from him. Shame heats my face over my lack of control.

Humans aren't supposed to act this way. We're supposed to remain in control of our baser urges—even kissing is frowned upon—and those who struggle are given extra hormone suppression shots. Frequent and careless fornication can lead to disease and unplanned pregnancies, along with a host of other problems a worldship with dwindling resources cannot handle.

But Tornn wants to copulate with me frequently, and he definitely wants to plant his seed in my womb. That's the whole point of this. That's why I was given to him as a bride. As payment.

He kneels briefly to remove my slippers, then rises and cups my face, settling his intense, purple gaze on me. "We need to remove your dress now, sweet human. It'll be easier for me to frisk you if you're unclothed."

Chapter 4

TORNN

Ellie doesn't protest as I reach to remove her shimmering gown. She cooperates fully, lifting her arms up as I pull the garment over her head. I toss the gown aside and step back to admire the loveliness of her curvy form.

She's wearing undergarments, of course. Panties and a bra—items I've heard most human females tend to wear. My cocks shift as I imagine stripping off the unnecessary coverings and revealing her naked body to my gaze.

The scent of her arousal remains strong in the air, and I can't help but breathe deeply of her perfumed excitement. My mouth waters at the prospect of licking her pussy.

One. She only has one pussy, I remind myself. Darrvason females have two, just as they possess two wombs. But according to our top physicians, the difference will not be a hindrance when it comes to procreating with the human females.

My blood heats as I envision myself pounding her with one cock until I erupt deep inside her, then immediately shoving my unspent shaft into her and claiming her all over again. She will be sore and dripping with my essence by the time I'm finished with her.

But I won't selfishly take my pleasure of her without giving anything in return. I plan to stroke her to completion, to caress the tiny button her people call a *clit* until she shatters to pieces. I've committed every detail of the physicians' report on human female physiology to memory, and I will use that knowledge to my advantage.

"You are beautiful, Ellie," I say, meaning it. My gaze falls to a strange dark splotch on the side of her stomach, and I move closer and trail my fingers over it. It's the size of a fist. A fading bruise? Rage boils inside me. "Who did this to you?"

"It's just a birthmark," she says in a worried tone, and my anger instantly cools. "I was born with it, and I have a few more on my back. I'm sorry if they bother you. We have the technology to remove birthmarks, but my-my father used to say they made me special. Perhaps it's silly, but as a child I believed him, and I always refused to have them removed whenever a doctor would offer."

With my fingers still trailing over her flesh, I move around her to inspect her back, eager to glimpse the unique markings. I count five more birthmarks in varying shapes and sizes, and I take my time tracing them. Finally, I turn her to face me and give her a gentle smile.

"Your markings don't bother me, Ellie. I'm sure no one else in the universe has markings exactly like these." I tip her face up, forcing her to hold my gaze. "They add to your beauty." I nearly reel at the sweet reassurances that spill from my lips. Why am I so eager to calm her fears? *Convenience and necessity*, I tell myself, *and nothing more*. As the admiral of the Darrvason fleet, I work long hours and have great responsibility. I cannot afford distractions or entanglements. But I must perform my duty to the Darrvason Empire and procreate.

She inhales a shaky breath, and a look of relief crosses her visage. "Thank you for saying so, Tornn." Her eyes widen. "I mean, *Admiral* Tornn. Forgive me for the blunder."

"You're my wife," I say, pleased to hear my name on her lips yet again. Especially without my title preceding it. "You're my mate. When we are alone together, you may call me *Tornn*."

"And when we're not alone?" A hint of fear enters her blue gaze.

"When we're in the company of others, you must address me by my title. It's custom. Commanders, other leaders, and officers are always addressed by their titles. Using a first name without a title in public is considered disrespectful."

She frowns, then swallows hard. "If I accidentally

call you *Tornn* in public, without using your title, what-what will you do?"

"Little wife, you seem to have a preoccupation with punishment," I say. "Perhaps a demonstration is in order? Perhaps I ought to give you a taste of what to expect if you disobey me… perhaps I ought to take you over my knee and smack your bottom a few times."

She gasps and her eyes go wider. "But I haven't done anything wrong. And you haven't frisked me yet."

I caress a hand through her silken locks. "I can frisk you and spank you at the same time. In fact, it will make things easier when I must check your orifices for any contraband. If you're draped over my knee, sweet human, I can readily spread your legs and your bottom cheeks for inspection."

She whimpers and starts to shake her head, but quickly stops. She takes a deep breath, and I can tell she's struggling to submit. No doubt she thinks I'm barbaric for what I'm about to do to her, but I won't back down no matter how sweetly she begs.

I sit on the bed and draw her close, positioning her to stand between my spread thighs. She bows her head in a show of capitulation so lovely, another surge of warmth for her fills me to bursting. I try to push the unwanted tenderness aside but fail miserably. Perhaps once I rut her for the first time, the affectionate feelings will dissipate. I can only hope.

I reach for the front clasp of her bra. "This needs to come off. I must make sure you're not hiding any contraband under here. Also, when you've committed an offense and I must punish you, you'll be entirely naked when I do so. Do you understand?"

Once I remove her bra, I can't hold back a feral growl from leaving my chest. Star Gods, she's breath-takingly gorgeous. I squeeze her bra gently as I search for any hyposprays or weapons before tossing it toward her discarded gown.

"I'm not hiding anything," she says in a soft but beseeching tone. "I swear it. Also, I don't have a preoccupation with punishment. You-you don't have to spank me. We can, um, move on to… *other things*." She whispers the last two words as though they are scandalous, and my cocks thicken massively in my pants, to the point that I almost reach down to read-just myself.

"Other things?" I press, reveling in the flush that tints her cheeks a dark pink hue. "Define *other things*." I'm toying with her, and *fluxx* I'm enjoying every moment of it.

Her eyes flicker with annoyance, but only very briefly. "Mating," she says in an even fainter whisper. "I mean *mating*. Copulation. Whatever you want to call it."

There's an instant where I consider accepting her offer. I'm more than eager to be vibrating balls-deep inside her. But I quickly dash the idea aside. I must frisk her, and I believe it's also important that I spank her. Her numerous questions regarding punishment make me worry she has a mischievous side, and she needs to understand that I'm her master and she must always, *always* obey me.

As the admiral of the Darrvason fleet, I cannot have an errant female running about the ship. If I'm unable to control my own female, the emperor as well as my comrades would undoubtedly start to question my governance.

"There will be plenty of time for copulation," I reply as I tug at the waistband of her panties, "*after* I frisk you and redden your little ass. Now, these need to come down." I swiftly yank her panties to her knees. My gaze goes straight to her center, to the smooth folds that glisten with her arousal. My balls quiver, nearly in a full vibration, and my shafts throb so hard that not for the first time in Ellie's presence, I become pleasantly lightheaded.

I run my fingers over the thin fabric of her under-garment, making sure nothing dangerous is hidden within any secret seams. Then I push her panties to her ankles and help her step out of them. Beautiful. She's so *fluxxing* beautiful, a few moments pass where I find it difficult to form a coherent thought. All I can do is stare and drink in her loveliness.

Mine. She's all mine.

My mate forever.

After years of fearing I would never have a female to call my own, the Star Gods have finally blessed me with Ellie. There are very few Darrvason females left, so few that there was a point in time where my people believed in the impending extinction of our race.

Ellie is hope incarnate. All the human females are.

But she alone is *mine*, the woman I will keep and protect until the end of my days. I still can't shake the intensity of the calling I'd felt when I first laid eyes on her. A *knowing* deep in my soul that said, *this one. She's yours.*

As I reach for her slick, plump folds, she arches toward my hand with a needy whimper. She makes a frustrated noise soon after that I suspect is a result of her embarrassment over her inability to control her desires. Her delicious wantonness. I bite back a grin as I remember the hormone suppression shots and realize she's probably experiencing arousal for the first time.

I probe her gently, dragging one finger through the seam of her nether lips. She undulates her center with a moan and grasps onto my shoulders for support. I growl and lean closer to her sex, taking deep inhales of her delectable essence. The intoxicating slickness that tells me she's ready to be claimed. That she's aching to be filled up with my shafts.

"How do you feel right now, sweet human? I want to know what you're experiencing. Describe it." I continue stroking her lightly, though I don't penetrate her. Not yet. I'll save that for when she's over my knee with her thighs parted wide, her nether area fully exposed for my inspection.

She whimpers and gives me a pleading look. "I'm achy. So achy. And breathless. I never knew... never knew..." Her voice trails off and she tightens her grip on my shoulders.

I find the tiny button hidden within her folds and

swirl her moisture overtop it, applying increasing pressure as she squeals and jerks against my touch.

"I think it's time for you to go over my knee, sweet human," I say, eventually withdrawing my hand. "If you're cooperative while I frisk you, I might be inclined to rub your clit until you shatter. Would you like that? Would you like me to stroke you to a release while you're draped over my lap with your center spread wide?"

Her only response is a whimpering moan.

I pull her down over one knee and get her situated to my liking, with her bottom lifted high, her thighs parted enticingly. I don't place my free leg atop hers yet—I'll save that for if she struggles.

Heat pummels me at the prospect of restraining her as I frisk her and swat her ass, a heady rush of power tempered by a protective desire to guide her in the proper ways of being a wife.

I reach for her bottom and boldly splay her cheeks apart. Her pussy lips are now spread open, revealing the sweetness hidden within, but my gaze is also drawn to her tiny puckering hole. It winks at me as though begging to be explored.

"Will you be an obedient wife as I search your orifices for contraband, Ellie?" I tap at her engorged clit. It's grown noticeably since I first touched it while she was standing in front of me.

"Yes, please, I-I'll be good."

"For your sake, I hope so. It would be a pity if I had to withhold an orgasm from you. Be a good little female and I'll allow you to come very soon."

Chapter 5

ELLIE

BLISSFUL AGONY SWEEPS THROUGH ME. ALL I CAN think about is the fervent aching in my core. Why won't it stop? Is it because I haven't had a *release*? I've heard of orgasms and the various names they go by, though I don't quite understand what they are.

Will stroking my clit truly help me feel better?

God, I can only hope.

Not to be dramatic, but it sort of feels like I'm dying.

My face heats as Tornn spreads me even wider. I try to remain still as he begins to insert one thick finger into my center, gliding in with careful, slow pumps, in and out, then deeper with the next drive. I gasp for air as he swirls his digit in a futile search for a hidden weapon or hypospray.

His touch elicits a quaking rush of pleasure, but it

soon builds to more frustration because something hovers out of reach. A sensation that tugs at me but won't quite come. Desperate to quench my desires, I wiggle slightly over his lap, inadvertently grinding my center over the hard bulge in his pants.

His two cocks.

Well, I think there are two of them. He never specified how many he possesses, just that there's more than one. God help me if there are three or four.

A deep vibration reaches me and rushes through my center. And holy fuck—it's coming from his pants. I'm no expert, but I don't think dicks are supposed to vibrate. A wave of apprehension jolts through me.

I'm in way over my head.

I hope he's patient when it comes time to bed me. I hope he doesn't become angry when he realizes I'm utterly inexperienced. I know the mechanics of sex from reading banned books I've gotten my hands on over the years, but the descriptions in the illicit romance novels always left me with more questions than answers.

At last, he withdraws his finger from my center, apparently satisfied that I'm not hiding anything. Mourning the loss of his touch, I release a desperate moan. But a second later, he nudges at my back hole. *Oh God oh God oh God.*

I tense up. I know I'd promised to cooperate, but I can't help it. The action he's about to take is so taboo, I can scarcely believe he truly intends to penetrate me *back there*.

"Naughty naughty," he says in a scolding tone.

"Relax your bottom hole, sweet human, and let me inside. I suspect you're very tight back here, and I promise I'll make it quick."

"I-I'm trying," I gasp out. "Please don't be angry. I'm just so nervous about you touching me there. It isn't proper. You shouldn't even look at this part of me."

"I'm your husband." That's all he says, as though his status as my husband is reason enough for him to claim every little part of my body. In his culture, I suppose it is.

Heated flushes rush through me as he presses at my forbidden entrance. The aching in my core doesn't cease. It gets stronger by the second, and moisture soon escapes to trickle down my inner thighs.

He finally breaches my snug hole, pushing a fingertip inside. Or maybe it's his whole freaking digit. I don't know. It feels awfully huge, even though the movement is slight. The pressure of the fullness isn't painful, but it's not exactly comfortable.

My feelings of exposure and vulnerability heighten, and I'm once again reminded that I'm completely at Admiral Tornn's mercy. Whatever he wants to do to me, I'll never be able to stop him.

But the longer his finger remains submerged in my back hole, the less uncomfortable it becomes. It's not long before I start to enjoy the exquisite fullness, and I swear my clit starts to throb in tune with my rapidly beating heart.

"Just a bit deeper, and then we'll be done. You're being a good little female," he says in a praising tone.

"I appreciate your cooperation in this matter. Your obedience pleases me beyond measure, and I intend to reward you once I'm finished inspecting this tight bottom hole of yours."

I barely hear him over the pounding of my pulse in my ears. Ecstasy floods me as he shoves deeper, and I don't understand why the indecent act is causing my clit to throb harder as my entire body quivers with desire.

Yes, surely I'm about to die. Whatever he's doing to me can't be normal. Any moment now, my heart will most definitely explode. That is, if my pussy doesn't combust first.

"There. My finger is fully submerged in your back hole. I don't think you're hiding anything, but let me do one more thing…" His voice trails off and he soon swirls his digit inside me.

Oh. Sweet. Lord.

I momentarily leave my body.

The fullness is too much. The throbbing in my nether parts becomes pure anguish. I struggle to breathe. When I try to move, Tornn places his free leg atop my slightly flailing ones, securing me over his lap as he invades my bottom hole with his massive finger, holding me captive for his thorough inspection.

I don't understand the waves of submission that keep surging over me, the odd but overwhelming need I have to please my new husband, to comply with his demands. Where is it coming from? It's a feeling that's so strong it seems almost… innate. Like a long-buried instinct that's only risen to the surface now that my alien mate has finally taken possession of me.

"No contraband. Good little female." With great care, he withdraws his finger from my bottom. Then he places this hand at the small of my back and touches my pussy with his other hand.

I tremble with need as he strokes my clit, applying the perfect amount of pressure.

Oh God. Oh yes. More. Please more.

I moan and writhe over his lap, allowing the unfamiliar urges to flow through me. Inviting the pleasure he's bestowing.

Desperate for the release he promised me, even though I'm not certain what it'll feel like or if it will alleviate my distress.

He dips a finger into my core and spreads more wetness over my throbbing button, then resumes caressing my clit with increasingly fast strokes. Blissful pressure builds and builds, until suddenly I'm truly dying, falling into an abyss of pleasure so great, I can't stop moaning and whimpering and undulating against his hand.

I'd thought I left my body only moments ago, but now I'm truly rising above myself, soaring to the stars that hover in open space beyond the *Haxxal*. My head buzzes, wind rushes past my ears, as I reach the sweetest rapture I've ever known.

And then suddenly I'm turned over on Tornn's lap, and he's cradling me against him, stroking my hair as he murmurs into my ear. I don't understand what he's saying, and it takes me a few seconds to realize he's speaking in the Darrvason tongue. The deep, guttural words fall over me, blanketing me in comfort. In safety.

Eventually, I float back into my body, and his warmth surrounds me further. I realize my head is leaning against his chest, and I can clearly hear his beating heart. His familiar scent grounds me in the present, reminding me that I'm really here and this isn't a dream.

I try to resist the comfort he's offering me. I try to remind myself that he pretty much bought me. Fuel, repairs, and navigational assistance in exchange for a wife.

Does he view me as his property?

Yes, I want the alliance to succeed, but that doesn't mean I have to enjoy the process. It doesn't mean I need to be happy about the part I'm playing.

I had a *fiancé*, an entire life planned out… and suddenly it was ripped away from me. I'm still not over the shock of being told I would be given to a Darrvason male.

Captain Warren could've at least asked for volunteers instead of handpicking the particular women he'd chosen. Instead, he'd taken the cruelest, most self-serving path possible when it came to selecting brides.

"You're drenched between your thighs, sweet human," Tornn says, reaching down to squeeze my center. "Before I administer your spanking, I'm going to get you all cleaned up. Let me set you on the bed for a moment while I fetch a damp cloth for your nether area."

He lifts me as though I weigh nothing and places me on the bed, laying me on my back. My knees are bent, my legs parted, and though I know I'm shamefully exposed, I don't have the energy to cover myself. So, I remain in place while he ventures to what I assume is a bathroom. I hear water running, and when I peek open my eyes and turn my head, I have a clear view of him washing his hands.

He peers through the doorway, his heated purple gaze searing me like a brand. Yes, he must view me as his property. I can see it in his eyes. The sure knowledge of his possession.

Despite my utter fatigue, I blush furiously under his penetrating stare, and the pulsing remnants of my powerful orgasm reignite. Decadent pulsations stir between my thighs, a faint echo of the intense pleasure he'd just inflicted upon me.

He grabs a cloth from a rack and runs it under the sink, then hurries to my side. I try to move when I realize his intentions—he wants to physically wipe the moisture from between my thighs. But I'm so weak in the aftermath of the release, that I can't quite move yet.

My face burns as he delves the cloth to my aching center and carefully wipes away my arousal. He even drags the damp cloth along the insides of my thighs. My legs tremble as he tends to me, and though I'm terribly embarrassed by what he's doing, there's a part of me that swoons. All things considered, his actions are sort of sweet.

He's taking care of me.

"There you go," he says in a voice that's almost warm. "All clean. My sweet human."

Sweet human.

For a reason I can't fathom, I like when he calls me that. It's an endearment. Like a pet name. In some of the romance novels I've secretly read over the years, some of the heroes and heroines had pet names for each other. I always thought the custom strange, but to my surprise, I find I like it now that I'm on the receiving end.

Nathan never called me by any endearments. Sadness pangs in my chest, and I don't understand why. Only that thoughts of him leave me conflicted.

Once Tornn finishes cleaning me, he traipses to the bathroom and tosses the cloth somewhere out of my vision. He returns immediately and sits beside me. Before I can process what's happening, he lifts me and guides me over his lap again.

My heart races.

Oh God. Oh no.

He's going to spank me.

He wants to give me a taste of what to expect if I ever earn a true punishment from him. A whimper drifts from my throat as I fear he's going to whip me. But he doesn't appear to have a belt or a strap of any sort. A small measure of relief fills me, but it soon vanishes as he cups my bottom with one large hand.

I recall how quickly he'd grabbed my suitcase, and unease tightens in my gut. He's fast and built of pure muscle and probably doesn't need a belt or a strap to make his point.

This is going to hurt. Badly. I know it.

I pull in a deep breath and brace myself, but he doesn't strike me immediately, and I soon have no choice but to resume breathing as normally as I can. Anticipation skitters through me as he commences rubbing my butt, moving from cheek to cheek and back again.

His hand is large and warm, his touch strangely intimate. Possessive. I can't shake the feeling that he truly owns me. Never mind that we haven't physically joined our bodies yet.

It's like I know there's already no going back. No chance I'll ever live on the *Jansonna* again. No chance I'll marry Nathan. I'll probably never see him again. And my mother and sister... I push thoughts of them aside because it's just too fucking painful.

A sense of vulnerability settles over me. I'm stripped of all my defenses and feeling so goddamn emotional right now that it's a wonder I'm not crying.

What will Tornn think if I break down in tears? Will he think I'm sobbing because I'm afraid or in pain?

"Shh," he says in the gentlest tone he's used thus far. "It's all right, sweet human."

I haven't made any noise that I'm aware of, but his tenderly spoken words wash over me, steeping me in an unexpected state of comfort and safety.

His hands leave my bottom, only for his fingertips to dance over the seam of my pussy lips. I lift my center to meet his touch. I can't help it. The fervent ache has returned to my core, and I'm desperate for another climax.

If I'm obedient while he swats my butt, will he grant me a second release? I can only hope, and I vow that I'll be on my best behavior. No matter how badly it hurts. No matter how embarrassing it is that I'm draped over my new husband's lap about to receive a spanking.

He skims my clit but doesn't apply any pressure, and it's all I can do to prevent a groan of frustration. I bite the inside of my cheek to keep from calling out.

"So slick and pink and wet," he says. "I cleaned you off moments ago, yet your private parts are already gleaming under a fresh sheen of your arousal. Tell me, little Ellie, are you aching again? Is your clit throbbing?"

I want to scream. I want to dive off his lap and shake a censorious finger at him for pointing out my helpless state of need. I can't control my urges; they keep coming as naturally as breathing. Yet he's basking in my desperation, taking pleasure in the fact that I'm soaking wet and quaking with need even as he prepares to smack my bottom.

He withdraws his hand from my clit and gives my left cheek a firm, resounding swat. The sudden impact stuns me, and the sting instantly spreads, the pain so much worse than I expected. "Answer me," he says in a sharp, commanding tone.

"Yes, I-I'm aching again, and my clit is throbbing." My voice breaks over the last few words, and I'm certain my face has never felt so hot. I imagine if I looked in a mirror, my entire visage would be bright red.

"If you're a good little female during your spanking," he says, his long fingers venturing close to my bottom hole as he caresses my ass, "I'll bring you to another release once we're finished. Submit to me as gracefully as you can, sweet human, and you'll be rewarded."

Before I have time to process his statement, he lifts his hand and brings his flattened palm down across both my cheeks. The sting takes my breath away.

Chapter 6

TORNN

AFTER I DELIVER THE SECOND SMACK, I PAUSE AND RUB Ellie's bottom. I can't resist the action. I want to touch her heated flesh and watch her puckering back hole wink at me as I pull one of her cheeks to the side. I can't help but wonder about that tiny, snug entrance of hers.

If I train her properly, perhaps with a set of plugs in increasing size, will she eventually manage to accept one of my cocks in her ass?

The idea of claiming her with both my cocks at the same time leaves me sweltering with need. Perspiration trickles down my temple. My vision blurs and my shafts pulse in the confines of my pants, my scrotum vibrating at full speed.

Satisfaction fills me as I lift my hand from her ass

and examine the redness marring her flesh. I swat her again, a bit lighter this time, my palm covering her entire bottom. More redness blooms, and I continue spanking her, watching as she squirms slightly and her thighs part wider, revealing the gleam of her increasing arousal.

Her movements are so faint that I couldn't call it disobedience. Besides, I can't deny I'm enjoying her movements. Each time she wiggles around, she rubs against my raging hard appendages. The friction is driving me mad with longing.

I want to flip her onto the bed, grasp her hips, and plunge deep into her wetness. I want to hold her down and pound her until she screams herself hoarse in the throes of a pulsating climax. A vision of her laying on the bed, panting breathlessly in the aftermath of our first mating session as my seed leaks from her core, causes my blood to heat to feverish levels.

I give her three more smacks, bringing the count to twenty moderately hard blows delivered to her little bottom. Just enough to leave her sore and red for a while. Enough to show her what she can expect if she ever earns a real punishment at my hand.

She's breathing hard, but I don't think she's crying. I listen carefully as I resume rubbing her ass. Eventually, her breathing starts to regulate, and she emits a sigh that's tinged with relief. No doubt she's thankful the demonstration has come to an end.

"Should you ever disobey me, Ellie, or show me disrespect, you can expect a much longer, much more severe thrashing." I pause, allowing my words to settle over her. "I also have no tolerance for lies. If you ever lie to me, sweet human, I won't hesitate to take a whip to your bottom. I'm your master, and you are not permitted to keep any secrets from me."

She tenses and sucks in a rapid breath, though she gradually relaxes as I continue caressing her punished cheeks.

I tuck her hair behind an ear, better revealing the side of her face, allowing me to glimpse her expression. She glances over her shoulder, peering at me with adorably pleading eyes as she lifts her bottom to meet my hand.

Her thighs fall wider apart, and the scent of her arousal heightens in the air, the sweetest perfume I've ever inhaled. I muse that I could get drunk on the scent of her alone, that with one brief glance I could lose myself in the very essence of her soul, I could *fluxxing* drown.

As warmth swells in my chest, I turn her over on my lap and cradle her in my arms, keeping one hand on her bottom, cupping her heated cheeks and occasionally squeezing them.

Our eyes meet and I don't understand why the moment lasts and lasts, seeming to transcend time itself.

To my amazement, the ancestral markings on my chest start tingling. I know what it means—or rather, what it's *supposed* to mean—but it can't be possible. Ellie is human. There is no way a traditional

Darrvason mating bond will ever form between us. No way she'll wear my ancestral markings on her arms.

But as I peer down at her and stroke her hair and squeeze her freshly-spanked buttocks, a fierce possessiveness for her ignites inside me.

All I can think about is claiming her.

Ravishing her to completion.

Because if I cover her with my scent, filling her thoroughly with my seed, she'll be protected even without the ancestral markings. No other Darrvason male would dare walk too close to her, let alone touch her.

Not that I have any plans to allow her to leave my quarters until we've copulated at least fifty times. I reason that will be enough to keep all other males away.

I have clear memories of newly mated females in my village being stolen away because their mate's scent wasn't strong enough to dissuade other males—because the female's husband let her roam too freely too soon. Before he fully saturated her with his masculine essence *and* before the ancestral markings had a chance to appear on her arms.

I remember the beating of drums that would precede *lahhkda*—a battle to the death between the first male and the challenging one. I remember the roar of the spectators and the blood spilling in the streets. I also remember my father making me watch every moment of the fighting as he lectured me on the proper way to keep a wife safe.

It seems like a lifetime ago since I traversed the

streets of the village I grew up in, and an unexpected melancholy pangs in my chest. I'm quick to push it away. There is no point in ruminating over the past. My village is gone, and I'm no longer the small, curious child I once was.

I'm a respected leader charged with the responsibility of guiding what's left of the Darrvason Empire to safety. I'm the admiral who is trying to prevent the very extinction of my people.

I remove my hand from Ellie's bottom, allowing her to sit more comfortably on my lap. She squirms over my hardness and her breath hitches. So does mine. Our eyes meet and I delve a hand between her thighs.

"I promised you another climax if you behaved during your spanking, didn't I?"

Her only response is a whimper, then she shifts on my lap, parting her legs further to allow my explorations. I dip one digit into her core before drawing her moisture overtop her bulging clit. She quivers and inhales a sharp breath.

My fully erect shafts throb beneath her bottom, my balls vibrate faster, and I regret that I'm still wearing pants.

I circle her little button, gradually building speed and pressing down harder. She moans and leans into my chest as her thighs tremble. Her sweet, pungent essence fills my lungs, and I release a low growl.

"Tornn?"

"Yes?"

"The vibrations in your pants... um, is that your

cock? I mean, your *cocks*?" Her eyes roll back in her head as I increase the strokes to her clit. A series of keening whimpers drift from her throat.

"No, sweet human, that isn't my cocks you feel vibrating. It's my scrotum."

Her eyes widen and she freezes. "Your balls actually vibrate?"

I lift one eyebrow at her, amused by her apparent shock. "Yes. When I'm aroused, my balls vibrate. I believe that while we are copulating, it will enhance your pleasure." If she enjoys having my fingers rubbing her sensitive little button, surely she'll like it when I thrust into her from behind, allowing my vibrating scrotum to smack against her swollen clit.

She flushes. "I must admit, that is surprising to me."

"I take it human males don't possess vibrating balls?" I ask wryly as I dip into her core to spread additional moisture over her nubbin.

She exhales a shaky breath and gives me a nervous look. "I'm not entirely certain, though I don't think human males have vibrating balls. I must confess that I don't have any, um, sexual experience, but in the illicit books I've read that describe intimate encounters, I never saw any mention of a vibration." She stares at me with a tense expression, as if anxious her reply might anger me.

"If you're worried I'll be disappointed that you have no experience, you can put those fears to rest. After learning about the hormone suppression shots all humans aboard the *Jansonna* are given, I assumed any bride I claimed would be delightfully innocent. I'm eager to teach you all you need to know, eager to instruct you in the ways of husbands and wives. Now, close your eyes and let the pleasure wash over you. Come for me, sweet human."

Chapter 7

ELLIE

DELICIOUS PRESSURE COILS IN MY CENTER, BUT AT least this time I know what to expect. I know I'm not actually dying, and I'm eager to experience the quaking bliss of a release.

This climax hits me harder than the first one, and I cry out as I clutch Tornn's shirt and ride the waves of ecstasy to the very end.

"Good little female," he says, running a hand up and down my back.

His balls are still vibrating beneath me, and then there's the massive bulge of his shafts to consider. I still haven't worked up the courage to ask exactly how many cocks he has. I suppose I can wait and find out when the time comes for him to claim me.

Anticipation hums through my insides, a heated

tingle coupled with a fresh pulsing ache between my thighs.

My core is completely drenched, and my face grows hotter as I wonder if Tornn plans to grab another damp cloth and clean me up again.

When will we mate? In a few minutes? Later this evening?

Nerves swarm me even as the prospect of being claimed by the handsome alien admiral causes my clit to resume throbbing. I can't help but wonder if I'll always feel like this around him. Unsettled and excited and unable to control my newly discovered urges.

He pulls back to stare down at me. "Ellie, I would like to——"

A steady buzzing noise interrupts him, and he says something terse in his native tongue that I suspect is a curse word. He lifts his right arm and I notice he's wearing a wrist comm that's flashing and buzzing. He glances at the tiny screen with a fierce scowl that sends a quiver of fear through me.

He sighs and lifts me briefly, setting me on the bed beside him, then runs a hand through his dark locks. "I regret that I must visit the medical bay, though I hope to return to you soon." He stands and reaches for my hand, helping me up.

Worry tightens in my stomach. "Is Paddax okay?" I pray his condition hasn't deteriorated, or worse... I can't complete the thought.

"I'm not certain, but the lead physician has requested my presence. I know he wouldn't bother me if it wasn't important. Especially today of all days."

I feel like he knows more but doesn't want to tell me. Not that I can blame him. We just met. We barely know one another. He probably hasn't decided whether he can trust me yet. I hope I can trust him. I think of my uncle, his first mate, and all the sleazy, power-hungry assholes on the command team. *God, please don't let Tornn be like them.*

Tornn leads me into the bathroom and gestures at a large tub. "You may bathe in my absence, and you are free to get dressed afterward. I am uncertain how long I'll be. Please make yourself comfortable in my quarters. If you get hungry, there's a food replicator in the kitchen." His demeanor has turned somewhat cold. Overly formal. As though the intimacies we just shared mean nothing to him.

As though I mean nothing to him.

My heart sinks, and I instantly feel like the biggest fool. I remind myself that he needs me for one purpose and one purpose only—procreation. For the rest of our lives, I'll likely be little more than a vessel to him.

"Thanks," I finally reply. "I'll be fine while you're gone."

He takes a step back and nods. Then he turns and strides out the automatic door of his quarters. The door closes behind him, and I wonder if it'll open for *me* if I approach it. I'm not planning to make a run for it—and honestly, where the hell would I go anyway? I'm on his ship and I don't know my way around. But I can't ignore the temptation to test the door.

Increasingly curious, I wrap a towel around myself,

wincing as the fabric rubs against my sore bottom, and traipse over to the door. But when I walk directly up to it, the damn thing doesn't budge. My pulse accelerates.

He told me I wasn't his prisoner, yet I can't help but feel like one.

Especially when I'm locked in his quarters.

Apparently, I'm not allowed to leave until he's ejaculated inside me multiple times, enough to cover me in his scent so no other Darrvason male tries to steal me.

I turn and look out the massive viewscreen, my eyes pausing on the *Jansonna*. After the *Haxxal's* docking tunnel disconnected from *Jansonna's* airlock, the human worldship drifted further away, taking up position in the center of the Darrvason fleet. I can see the outline of the larger viewscreens on the upper decks, and I try to figure out which one belongs to my family, but sigh with disappointment when I'm not successful.

I start to head back to the bathroom, but a huge painting on the wall catches my attention. It's a depiction of a breathtakingly gorgeous alien city that rests in a valley. The buildings are constructed of what appears to be multi-colored stones. The roofs are green, teeming with lush gardens. In the distance, there are sparkling lakes and huge snow-capped mountains.

Is this a painting of the city Tornn calls home? Where is his planet located? It's beautiful, and a sense of longing reverberates in my chest. *Land*. Real land.

My whole life, I've been waiting for the day the *Jansonna* would reach a habitable planet and we could finally disembark the worldship. So many times, I've imagined the moment I would first set foot on a planet, dreaming about how solid and permanent the ground would feel beneath my feet.

I swallow past the burning in my throat. The *Jansonna* houses over fifty-thousand humans. It's a feat of technology, or so my father always said. But it's never felt like home. Not really. Because we were taught it wasn't enough. Because we knew if we didn't reach a habitable planet before we depleted our resources, we would be done for. We would perish in the cold darkness of space.

After tearing my gaze from the painting, I continue to walk around Tornn's spacious quarters. The furniture is sparse, though his living space doesn't seem too sterile. There are more landscape paintings that add color to the various rooms I walk through, as well as metallic artwork that's attached to the walls.

I open all the drawers I can find, only to discover most are empty. Tornn doesn't appear to have many belongings, aside from a closet filled with black clothing and boots. There are no photographs of family members or friends. No mementoes. But maybe his people don't care about those things.

Once I'm finished snooping, I hurry back to the bathroom and draw myself a bath. Fortunately, the controls are easy to figure out, and I manage to get the tub filled with warm, soapy water.

I ditch my towel, step into the tub, and start to sink

down in the water. I hiss as my sore bottom meets the hot water, reinvigorating the sting of my spanking, but after a moment the pain recedes and I manage to sit down.

It's been ages since I've enjoyed a real bath with steaming water. The *Jansonna* has been dealing with water shortages for years, and even wealthy families like mine who live in luxurious upper deck quarters must ration their water usage and consumption. That means nothing but freezing cold, one-minute showers.

My mind wanders as I lounge in the tub. Tornn's been gone for about twenty minutes, and though I try not to worry about the reason for his absence, I can't help it. I finally allow myself to complete the thought I couldn't finish earlier…

If Paddax dies, what will that mean for the alliance? What will it mean for the woman who injected him with the harmful substance? I try to remember all the faces from our group of thirty. I don't know all their names, but I'd recognized most of them from school and social activities. Those who'd spent time in the brig were familiar since it's a very public event when an individual on the *Jansonna* is sentenced to serve time away from society. Trials, like executions, are broadcast on every available screen on the ship.

I sigh and resolve that I'll find a way to visit the human woman who's currently in the *Haxxal's* brig. Once I'm permitted to leave Tornn's quarters, I'll speak with her and discover why she attacked her mate. Maybe if I can convince her to apologize, everything will be okay.

A dark thought enters my mind. What if she was defending herself against Paddax? What if he was trying to hurt her and she simply fought back? The hypospray filled with poison (or whatever it was filled with that caused illness) could've been her insurance plan. Maybe Paddax was rough and tried to force himself upon her. Maybe she had no choice.

Shit. I run a hand through my hair, then dunk my entire head under the water. After I resurface, I wipe the water from my face and try to stop myself from thinking the worst of the Darrvasons. I know so little about them that maybe it's not fair to paint any of them as villains.

All I know about them is from scant information Nathan has shared with me. As a security officer, he's observed several meetings between the command team and the aliens from afar as he stood guard in the docking bay.

They're more technologically advanced than us and possess an impressive amount of weaponry. They're currently exploring this sector of space and aren't entirely familiar with it, but they claim to have discovered several nearby planets that hold promise for humankind, and they recently deployed probes to those planets.

Beyond this information and the fact that they're low on females, the Darrvasons are a mystery to me. How far away is their homeworld? How long have they been exploring this sector?

They found us. They came upon the *Jansonna* so quickly one day, their fleet bolting out of hyperspace directly in front of the bridge's viewscreen, evading our sensors and taking the entire worldship by surprise.

At the time, we were dead in the water and desperately trying to make repairs on the *Jansonna*. Unable to defend ourselves, we'd expected them to attack or perhaps board us to steal our resources. We hadn't expected them to ask what our females looked like and demand we send them blood samples.

The meetings started soon after that, the negotiations between the Darrvason leaders and *Jansonna's* command team, and before I knew it, my uncle was informing me that I would be given to an alien male for breeding purposes.

Breeding purposes. Yes, he'd used that exact phrase, and I suspect he'd said it to frighten me. If he weren't such a bastard, he might've gently explained that I was to become the wife of a Darrvason male.

I think of the banned romance novels I've read over the years, the many plot lines that involved forced marriages. I never imagined it would happen to me. I never imagined that sort of thing could occur in real life. Thousands of years ago, yes, but not at this point in the history of humankind.

I drain the tub and commence rinsing myself off under a water spray that's so intense, it feels like a pleasant massage on my back and my scalp. I sigh with contentment. The Darrvason's barbaric tendencies aside, I could get used to the amenities on this ship.

Just as I step out of the tub with a large towel wrapped around my body and another wrapped around my head, I hear footsteps approaching. The bathroom doesn't contain a door, and I peer into the open area of Tornn's quarters as my heart races and warmth quakes between my thighs.

We haven't mated yet. Surely, he intends to rectify that soon.

His large form suddenly fills the doorway, and I gulp hard at the unreadable look he's wearing. I can't tell whether he's angry or aroused. My bottom cheeks quiver as I recall every moment of the spanking he'd given me earlier, how his large hand had bounced off my stinging flesh. For some reason, this causes the pulses in my core to throb harder.

He crooks a finger at me. "Come here, little female."

Chapter 8

TORNN

My blood heats as Ellie approaches. Her skin holds a flushed glow in the aftermath of her bath. She's wrapped in a towel and the perfumed scent of soap clings to her, but I can easily detect the slickness of her arousal beneath that fragrance.

Savage desires pulse through my veins as the urge to conquer her becomes all-consuming. But alongside my baser instincts, I also experience a gentle yearning that I don't understand. Then my ancestral markings start to tingle again.

Fluxx. What sort of trick is my body playing on me? A heartbond between a human and a Darrvason isn't possible. It's what I've always been taught—that Darrvasons can't enjoy a heartbond with an otherworldly being, even if we're sexually compatible with the alien.

I draw myself up taller and scowl at my human female. Her throat bobs as she swallows hard, and her tiny hands, which are clutching the towel that's wrapped around her, begin shaking. Guilt settles over me. She's shaking and her eyes are wide with fear because of the angry way I'm looking at her. I curse myself inwardly. I want her obedience, but I don't want her quaking with terror whenever I come near.

With great effort, I school my features into neutrality. At least, I think I'm maintaining a blank expression. I don't think I can summon warmth at this moment. Not when I'm furious and shocked by what I just learned in the medical bay. Perhaps I shouldn't have returned to Ellie until my rage had calmed.

"Is Paddax all right?" she whispers as she finishes approaching. She comes to stand directly before me, struggling to maintain a grip on the towel as her hands tremble harder.

"He will survive," I say, then add, "but I do not wish to speak of him right now." Thankfully, the remaining males from the docking bay have all finished reporting back to Captain Varll, and none of their females were found in possession of any contraband. What happened with Paddax appears to be an isolated incident, but that doesn't negate the seriousness of it.

A highly sophisticated, fast-acting virus. That's what the female injected him with. A virus that was no doubt intended to cause havoc among my crew. Fortunately, our doctors and scientists worked quickly in the medical bay to formulate and administer a vaccine to all who'd come into contact with Paddax after the injection.

I repress a growl and try to focus on the flecks of brown in Ellie's stunning blue eyes. The longer I stare at her and bask in her soft beauty, the calmer I start to feel, as though she's the cure for all that ails me. I reach for her, taking her shoulders in a gentle grip, drawing her closer. Calmness permeates me further.

My nostrils flare as I inhale her scent over and over again. She quivers as I place a finger under her chin, forcing her to hold my gaze. "I'm not angry with you, sweet human. You needn't be so afraid right now."

She exhales a rapid breath. "Well, I'm relieved your anger isn't directed at me. You look like you're ready to commit murder."

Perhaps I hadn't adequately rearranged my face as I'd hoped. I latch onto the warmth I'm experiencing for her and try to gentle my expression. "What about now?" I ask. "Do I look less severe?"

She nods, and a smile tugs at her lips. "Yes, you look less murderous now." And just like that, she stops shaking. Her sudden ease gratifies me more than I expected.

"Good." I clear my throat. "Did you enjoy your bath?" I hadn't suggested a bath because I thought her unclean, but because I knew the full magnitude of the damages aboard the *Jansonna* and figured she hadn't enjoyed a warm bath in some time.

"Oh yes, thank you," she replies in a gushing tone. "It was very relaxing, and I haven't felt this clean in ages." She flushes. "On the human worldship, we are only permitted one quick, cold shower every other day."

"You are free to bathe as often as you wish while aboard the *Haxxal*," I say. "We aren't experiencing any energy or water shortages." I release her chin and take a step back.

She inclines her head and says, "Thank you, again." Then she straightens and looks me directly in the eye. "There's something I would like to speak with you about. After I get dressed, that is. If you'll excuse me."

I finger the towel she's wearing. "Now that I've returned, there is no need for you to get dressed, sweet human, but I am willing to speak with you." I guide her into the bedroom, where I sit on a chair and pull her into my lap. The need to have her close is overpowering, and the second her bottom is pressed upon me, my shafts harden and my balls commence vibrating.

I untwist the towel from around her head, toss it aside, and slowly comb my fingers through her damp locks. Her breath hitches as she squirms on my lap, no doubt feeling the firm evidence of my arousal. The scent of her slickness remains heavy in the air.

"What is it you wish to speak with me about?" I ask, still drawing my fingers through her hair.

"It's about Paddax and his mate." She lowers her head, appearing penitent. "I know you don't wish to speak of him anymore, but I-I would ask for your help with something."

"My help?"

Her eyes move back to mine. "Please don't breathe a word of what the human woman did to Paddax to Captain Warren or anyone on *Jansonna's* command team." She places a hand on my chest. "Please. I beg you."

"Why?" I study her features and take note of the worry that abruptly clouds her eyes, as well as the trembling of her lips.

"Forgive me, but I prefer not to say why." She draws in a shaky breath and casts a frightful glance around the room, as though anxious someone might overhear her. "But I promise I'll do whatever you want if only you promise to keep the woman's actions a secret from my uncle. *Please.*"

I clutch her upper arms. "What will Captain Warren do if he finds out?" I ask in a commanding tone. "Tell me, little female. Right now. Explain yourself."

Her eyes go wide and she shakes her head, keeping her lips pressed together. Her refusal to answer me is shocking, and I consider flipping her over my knee. I consider thrashing her until she answers all my questions. But I hesitate at the continued fear in her eyes. So, I grip her arms harder and give her a slight shake instead.

"Tell. Me." The order escapes me as a thunderous growl.

Her face goes white, and she opens her mouth, though no words issue forth. Inexperienced with females, I am unsure whether to be more forceful or if it's gentleness that will inspire her to open up.

"Ellie," I say in a firm but also encouraging tone. "You must tell me."

Her eyes brim with moisture, and she nods. "Okay," she whispers. "Okay." She blinks rapidly and several tears cascade down her cheeks.

I release her arms and brush away the tears with my thumbs, uncertain why they bother me so much, and I have the sudden urge to rip Captain Warren apart with my bare hands. It's his fault she's upset—for a reason I can't yet discern, she's nervous about him finding out what happened to Paddax.

"My uncle warned me to be obedient and set a good example for the other human women," she says. "Logically, I know there was nothing I could've done to prevent the woman from attacking Paddax. Whoever she might be, I knew nothing of her plan and I don't know why she did it, but I can't help but worry that Captain Warren will somehow blame me. He said if I'm not a willing enough bride, or if I cause any trouble, he will reduce the rations my mother and sister receive and perhaps even withhold medical care or force them out of their quarters. I'm also willing to bet he threatened some of the other brides. If the woman who attacked Paddax has anyone left on the *Jansonna* that she cares about, my uncle will probably go out of his way to make them suffer."

It would be a miracle if I didn't snap Captain Warren's neck at the next meeting between our people. Rage simmers inside me that he would dare to threaten my bride or those she cares about, and I quickly formulate a plan to prevent her mother and sister from suffering.

I cup Ellie's face in my hands, allowing my thumbs to trail over the faint tear streaks on her cheeks. "You have nothing to fear, sweet human. I will make sure the captain can't seek revenge against your family or the families of the other brides. I give you my word."

A look of relief starts to cross her face, only for a spark of worry to enter her eyes anew. "I appreciate your help, Tornn, but how can you make such a promise? How can you remain apprised of my uncle's actions aboard the *Jansonna*?"

"Because I can easily make a surprise trip to the human worldship and pay your uncle a visit. If the filthy *rustolla* values his life, he will comply with my demands."

Chapter 9

ELLIE

I QUESTION TORNN FURTHER, TRYING TO EXTRACT details about what he plans to tell my uncle. About how he plans to threaten him. But my alien mate remains firmly tight lipped and keeps brushing my questions aside. Eventually, I give up questioning him altogether, though I'm filled with cautious hope that he'll follow through with his promise to protect the families of the brides. Including my mother and sister.

A smug sense of satisfaction fills me as I imagine Tornn threatening Captain Warren. For a moment, fear jolts through me as I realize my uncle will likely realize I've basically snitched on him to my new husband, but the anxiety just as quickly subsides. Because raw power radiates from Admiral Tornn, and there's no doubt in my mind that if he issues a threat, he'll follow through with it.

Gratitude swells in my chest as he drags his nose along my neckline, taking huge inhales of my scent. I'm touched that he's helping my family as well as the other brides' families. Perhaps the Darrvasons aren't as barbaric and unfeeling as I'd feared.

At some point as he continues smelling me, the towel becomes loose and slides down my body. I hastily attempt to cover myself, only for Tornn to grasp my hands and utter, "No," in that deep, growly voice of his.

Now that I no longer have to worry about my uncle (well, as long as Tornn's telling the truth), I realize I have more freedom when it comes to the admiral. I could resist him if I wanted to. I could refuse to mate with him tonight. While I might face Tornn's wrath if I'm disobedient, at least my family wouldn't suffer for my actions.

But as the huge alien presses his lips to my shoulder, placing a lingering kiss there, heated tingles sweep through me as a sense of surrender settles deep in my bones. A yearning unlike anything I've ever known grips me, causing my breaths to come shallow and quick.

I can't explain why, but I want to please Tornn. I want to submit to him and allow him to claim me. It doesn't make sense—I'm still in love with Nathan, aren't I? I try to summon his face in my mind, but the image is blurred and rapidly fades as Tornn starts nibbling on my ear.

A whimpering moan drifts from my throat. His teeth are so sharp, yet he's only gently biting me. He's not chomping down hard enough to draw blood. But the thrill of danger is there, the knowledge that he could hurt me if he wanted to. I take a deep inhale and lose myself in the sensations of arousal and longing, trusting that he won't cause me any harm.

The bulge in his pants feels huge, and his balls are vibrating hard, causing my clit to throb, and making it impossible for me to sit still. I keep squirming over his lap and rubbing myself against his hardness. Every so often, he growls into my ear, a deep animalistic noise that sends fresh pulses of heat racing to my pussy.

Without warning, he snarls and lifts me slightly so he can yank the towel out from under my bottom. He throws it to the floor, then settles his hands on my hips and holds me down upon his shafts, his pants the only barrier between us. My lips part on a moan as the vibrations to my clit intensify, but before I can take my next breath, his lips are pressed to mine and he's kissing me.

He releases my hips to cradle my head in his huge hands, his fingers digging into my scalp. A steady growl rumbles from him as his tongue delves into my mouth. My heart pounds in my chest. This is the second kiss of my life, and it's vastly different from the first one.

When Nathan and I first started dating, we decided we wanted to try kissing, never mind that it was frowned upon behavior. That kiss was quick and unremarkable. After satiating our mutual curiosity, neither of us ever instigated another one.

Tornn's kiss is almost violent compared to

Nathan's. It's savage and possessive, and my head spins as his tongue keeps tangling with mine. It's shocking to my innocent sensibilities, but I find I don't want him to stop, and it's not long before I'm sweeping my tongue into his mouth as I mimic his movements. His growls increase and so does the pace of vibrations underneath me.

Holy hell, I think I'm close to…

I tear my lips from his and cry out as waves of ecstasy pulse through my core. My eyes flutter shut. *Oh God.* I'm climaxing from the vibration of his balls alone. His hands aren't anywhere near my center.

When the last pulsing remnant of my release fades, I blink my eyes open and find Tornn is staring at me with a satisfied expression. His gaze is also heated, and I swear I feel his bulge growing even larger beneath my sore bottom.

He laces his fingers through my hair and gives a sharp tug. I gasp but don't try to pull away. His dominance enthralls me as I wonder what he's going to do next. Will he soon release his cocks from his pants and settle himself between my thighs?

"A third orgasm?" He gives me a somewhat scolding look, though I'm not certain if he's being serious. Then he lifts me off his lap and forces me to stand in front of him while he makes a show of inspecting his lap.

I gasp when I notice the large wet spot I've left on the front of his pants. And when I press my thighs together, I feel the moisture that's leaked from my core. The slickness that signifies my arousal. My face heats with shame and my pulse quickens.

His gaze lifts to my pussy and he reaches out, dragging a finger over my folds. I quiver at his touch and try to remain upright.

"So wet, sweet human, and your folds appear swollen. And your clit is so engorged that it's poking out from between your damp petals."

I don't know if he expects me to respond, but in any case, I can't find the words. Am I supposed to reciprocate his comments by remarking on his massive bulge or the intensity of his balls' vibrations? I don't know, and my throat is so dry, I doubt I could speak even if my life depended upon it.

He continues drawing his finger through my folds, spreading my moisture around, though he seems to be avoiding my clit on purpose. He comes close to touching it a few times, only to take a detour. Even though I just orgasmed, it's not long before the incessant ache returns, and I find myself longing for more. I want to sit on his lap again and ride the vibrations to completion.

Tornn cups my pussy and gives it a firm squeeze that has me whimpering. He holds my gaze and squeezes again. "Who owns this pussy of yours?"

I swallow hard. "You-you do."

His nostrils flare and his eyes darken. "That's right, sweet human, your pussy belongs to me. Now, bend over the bed and spread your legs wide. I intend to make use of my property."

Chapter 10

TORNN

I WATCH, ENRAPTURED, AS ELLIE NERVOUSLY COMPLIES with my order to bend over the bed. She gives me an uncertain look and opens her mouth as though to speak, but she soon presses her lips together, then turns and bends over the bed, situating herself to my liking with her thighs spread wide. Her glistening pink parts are fully on display, beckoning me to surge inside and pump her full of my seed.

The sight of her punished bottom sends fresh pulses of heat through my insides. Her cheeks are still deliciously red. My desire spikes. I like seeing the evidence of my discipline on her small but curvy ass, even if the spanking I'd given her had been a light one and the marks would likely soon fade. How I'd enjoyed having her over my lap as she whimpered and squirmed while I brought my flattened palm down across her quivering cheeks.

I rise from the chair and tear off my shirt, then make quick work of removing my boots and pants. My cocks spear outward, throbbing, and my scrotum continues its steady vibration.

As I approach my human bride, she peers over her shoulder and gasps. Her eyes go wide, and she immediately moves her thighs back together in a charming display of virginal apprehension.

I take my lower cock in hand, stroking it, while my upper shaft rests atop it, fully erect and protruding straight out from my body.

I approach Ellie and tap her bottom. "Spread your thighs."

"Will-will they fit?" she blurts, her wide eyes still focused on my appendages. She also keeps looking at the glowing ancestral markings that cover my upper chest, though she doesn't comment on them.

"Yes, sweet human, I assure you they will fit. But I'll only thrust one shaft into your center at a time. Perhaps eventually you will learn to take my upper length in your ass, but until I've trained you properly to accept a double pounding, I will only plunge into you with one cock at a time."

Some of the anxiety fades from her eyes, and she gives a brief nod before turning around and gripping the covers. I move closer and drag my lower cock through her moist folds several times, coating the tip of my shaft in her essence.

A mate. I can scarcely believe it. I'm about to

claim a female as my own. I release my shaft and caress my hands down the slender curve of Ellie's back, admiring her birthmarks. She shudders under my touch and her center bucks outward as she tries to press her pussy more firmly to my lower cock. My eager little bride.

"Are you aching to be filled up, sweet human?" As I continue trailing my hands up and down her back, I step forward and allow my lower appendage to press into her wet heat. She cries out and writhes against me, and it takes all my willpower not to surge into her depths. But not yet. When I ask her a question, I expect an answer.

I sigh and step away, then bring my hand cracking down on her left cheek. She gasps and tries to evade further chastisement, but I'm quick to administer an equally severe smack to her right cheek.

"Yes!" she finally answers. "Yes, I'm aching to be filled up."

I run my hands up her back again, and when I reach her long dark locks, I give them a hard yank in warning. "In the future, when I ask you a question, I expect an immediate answer. Failure to respond in a prompt manner will result in punishment. Do you understand?" I cup her bottom in one hand and give it a hard squeeze, no doubt reinvigorating the sting of the smacks I'd just delivered.

"Yes, I-I understand," she says, and I smile to myself at how quickly she responds this time.

I massage her bottom, moving from cheek to cheek, keeping my ministrations gentle. An erotic thrill shudders through me, making my shafts harden further and my balls vibrate faster.

There's no doubt in my mind that training her to be a proper, obedient wife will be the greatest pleasure I've ever known.

I probe the wetness between her thighs, and she suddenly opens herself to me, spreading her legs wide apart.

"Sorry," she murmurs. "I just remembered you asked me to spread wide for you. I-I got distracted by your huge, um, by your…" Her voice trails off and though I don't have a clear view of her face, I sense she's blushing.

I slowly insert two fingers into her center, testing her readiness to be filled up. She's soaking wet—ready to be rutted hard and fast. After withdrawing my digits, I align my lower shaft with her pussy and push until the tip is submerged inside her.

Tight. She's so *fluxxing* tight, my vision swirls.

Her whimpers and moans combine with my feral growls as I give another slight push. I pull out only to drive straight back inside, going a little deeper with this thrust. I grasp her buttocks, drawing her cheeks wider apart so I can glimpse that enticing, puckering hole of hers.

As I shove my lower shaft farther into her depths, my upper cock rubs along the crevice of her ass. Grasping her hips, I withdraw from her pussy again only to drive back inside. I continue in this manner until at long last I find myself fully seated in her tight, wet channel.

Reaching underneath her, I press my vibrating balls more firmly to her clit. She cries out and undulates her core against me, and I snarl and grasp her hips and start surging in and out of her, unable to hold back from giving her quick, vigorous thrusts.

The sound of flesh slapping flesh echoes in the room, and I peer down at our joined bodies, marveling at the physical act of our mating.

Mine mine mine.

I feel my ancestral markings tingle yet again, but I soon become so lost in the delirious pleasure of claiming my mate that I don't have the mental energy to ponder the meaning.

I tangle my fingers in her hair and tug until her back arches, which forces her to accept my lower shaft deeper than before. She groans and whimpers, and then her insides contract tightly around me.

"That's it, little female. Come for me." I thrust harder, my balls slamming into her clit with each rapid drive.

My climax hits me like a tidal wave. I growl through my release as my seed surges into Ellie's depths in a series of pulsating eruptions. *Fluxx.* Black dots dance in my vision, and I struggle for air.

Still panting, I gradually withdraw my spent appendage from my bride's swollen center. I step back and peer down at her folds, watching with primal satisfaction as my blue, translucent seed trickles from her core and slides down her inner thighs. While I like seeing my marks on her bottom, I *love* seeing my seed coating her flesh.

I experience the sudden urge to fist my upper shaft until I spend on her back or perhaps even her punished ass, but I quickly decide I want her pussy again. Even if she's sore. Even if she begs me not to.

She glances over her shoulder, giving me a confused look when I approach her with my upper cock in hand, aiming for her slick folds all over again.

"Tornn?" She whimpers and fists the covers in her grip.

"I'm not finished with you yet, sweet human. Be an obedient little bride and hold still as I pound you with my other shaft."

Chapter 11

ELLIE

IT'S DECADENTLY WARM AND THE BED IS SOFT. THERE'S a weight atop my back, but I'm too fatigued to turn over and discover what it is. Fragments of dreams fade in and out of my consciousness as I struggle to wake up.

My first alert thought is a question: Why am I not shivering?

Mornings on the *Jansonna* are the coldest part of the day. Most of the time when I awake, I can see white puffs of my breath. Blinking at my surroundings, I release a long exhale just to confirm the temperature isn't below freezing. Nothing.

Why is the wall a silvery shade? In my family's quarters, my bedroom walls are a dull light blue.

As I shift underneath the covers, I become aware of the soreness between my thighs...

And suddenly all my memories fall back into place.

I inhale a shuddering breath as I slowly turn to face Tornn. He has one arm draped over me, and as I face him, he makes a pleased growling sound in his sleep and pulls me closer.

We're married. Mated. Whatever you want to call it.

In his culture, I belong to him. Possibly forever. I don't know for certain, but I don't think Darrvoson couples ever split up. The word *mate* sounds very permanent. My heart races with panic, but I force in a few deep breaths and soon start to feel calmer. Maybe it's because my alien husband appears so peaceful while he's sleeping. He looks younger, the lines and angles of his face less severe.

I take a moment to study the strange glowing symbols that cover his upper chest. They remind me of the symbols in the *Haxxal's* docking tunnel. To my surprise, as I stare at the markings on Tornn's muscular chest, my upper arms began to itch and tingle. I scratch my arms until the discomfort fades.

My gaze travels to my mate's sensuous lips, and heated tremors besiege me as I recall all the times he'd kissed me throughout the night. His kisses had made me feel drunk and breathless and achy.

After watching Tornn for a few seconds and ensuring he's truly asleep, I lift the covers and peer at his male equipment. His two shafts are flaccid but still huge, and his scrotum is a big, textured round thing nestled under his appendages. His nether area is completely hairless, just as mine is.

About a week before we left the *Jansonna*, all the brides were encouraged to receive permanent hair removal treatments on our legs, nether area, and under arms. I wonder if the aliens requested it, or if the command team simply thought it would make us look more appealing to the Darrvasons.

I reach between my thighs and marvel at the smoothness. I'm still not used to it, and a flush covers my face as I recall how my bareness had heightened my sense of exposure while I was draped over Tornn's knee.

There's a growing ache inside me that's tinged with the pleasant soreness that comes from being thoroughly ravished. I almost moan when my fingers brush over my clit, but I stop myself just in time. I cast a worried look at Tornn but breathe a sigh of relief to find he's still sleeping.

I'm glad I woke up before him. After all that happened last night, I like having a few minutes to myself to collect my thoughts.

How *do* I feel, anyway?

Not terrible, I decide after a contemplative moment.

More than anything, I'm surprised by Tornn. There's definitely a savage side to him, and he's bossy as hell, but I don't get the sense that he's cruel. At least not when it comes to me.

He'd seemed angry when I confessed the threats my uncle had leveled against me and my family. But he wasn't angry with me. Instead, his fury was directed toward Captain Warren. And now he would ensure my uncle didn't harm the families of the Darrvason brides.

Relief and gratitude swell in my heart. Mom and Jenny will be okay. My uncle won't be able to reduce their rations or withhold medical care or evict them from their quarters. I gaze at Tornn, my throat burning with emotion. His promise to keep them safe means the universe to me.

I pray this compassionate act will be the first of many. If he shows me kindness on occasion, perhaps I won't be so miserable living among his people. Perhaps I won't constantly be heartsick over missing my family and Nathan.

There's no going back. No returning to my old life. So, I might as well try to make the best of my circumstances. Will it be possible to find happiness as a Darrvason bride?

I still have so many questions about the aliens' way of life. Like what rights (if any) do I have as a human female living among Tornn's people. How their children are raised. Where their homeworld is located. How long their lifespan is. My mind swirls as more questions surface, including whether or not I'll be allowed to have a job.

We'd stayed awake long into the night, but we hadn't done much talking. Unless Tornn's dirty talking counts. Warmth quakes in my center as I recall his naughtiest comments.

So slick and pink and wet. I cleaned you off moments ago,

yet your private parts are already gleaming under a fresh sheen of your arousal.

That's right, sweet human, your pussy belongs to me. Now, bend over the bed and spread your legs wide. I intend to make use of my property.

I'm naked under the covers. He won't permit me to wear clothing in bed, insisting that I will always sleep in the nude because he wants easy access to my nether parts. As I wiggle around a bit, I feel the slickness of my arousal gathering between my thighs. I instantly yank my hand away.

My stomach flips, and I try very hard to stop entertaining impure thoughts… I don't want my scent to wake him up. Furthermore, the idea of him opening his eyes and immediately detecting my arousal fills me with shame. I can't help it. The idea that sex is an indecent, barbaric act was instilled in me at an early age.

I glance around the bedroom for anything resembling a clock but don't see one. But it feels late in the morning, and a sense of wrongness falls over me that I'm still abed.

If I were still on the *Jansonna*, I would probably be getting ready for a day of teaching alongside my mother. Most education courses are self-guided, but we offered in-person lectures on the History of Earth and Humankind. The classes are on hold for the foreseeable future—my mother wanted to take a leave of absence after my departure.

My heart sinks. I worry she's mourning my loss as though I've died. She never quite recovered from the loss of my father and it's a cruel twist of fate that I would be ripped away from her only two years later. I hope Jenny can bring her comfort.

Thankfully, my eighteen-year-old sister is strong. She's one of those people who always knows the right thing to say, and whenever there's a crisis, she's quick to jump into action. She's also perpetually cheerful and never complains about anything, not even reduced ship-wide rations, cold water, or the freezing temperatures that often plague our shared quarters.

I send up a silent prayer of thanks that Jenny is too young to be selected as a Darrvason bride. But a second later, a terrible thought enters my mind.

She'll be nineteen in less than a year. What if it takes longer than that for the aliens to guide us to a habitable planet? It's possible Jenny might turn nineteen before we're settled on a new world, which means she could end up in the final group of brides.

I stare at Tornn, hoping his people will be quick about finding a planet for us. Hopefully the probes they recently deployed will confirm one of the nearby planets is indeed habitable.

I also can't help but wonder... if I believed Jenny was in danger of being selected as a Darrvason bride, would Tornn intervene at my request? Would he keep her off the list?

Maybe. If he cares about me and wants me to be happy.

Can I *make* him care about me? Do Darrvasons possess the capacity for love? Or do they only care about owning their females and forcing them to pop out baby after baby?

Tornn stirs in his sleep and his large purple eyes blink open. He appears instantly alert as he focuses on me.

I force a smile that doesn't feel very forced. Deep down, I want him to hold me in high regard because that's how it's supposed to work between husbands and wives. We're supposed to care about one another. Given the circumstances that brought us together, maybe that's a silly notion, but I can't help but yearn for his affection. For the kind of loving relationship my parents once enjoyed.

If we don't grow to care for one another, I fear my life will become incredibly lonely. I think of how many hours a day I spent with Nathan, talking, cooking together, watching banned movies from Earth that we didn't always understand, and simply enjoying one another's company. Now that companionship has been abruptly stolen from me, along with my family, and I don't like the emptiness that has followed.

I've lapped up the semi-tender looks and heated glances Tornn has sent my way like I'm starved for attention. Maybe my fear of being lonely is part of the reason I'm so eager to please him.

"Good morning, sweet human." His eyes are sharp, his expression one of suspicion.

"Good morning," I whisper.

Before I can take my next breath, he grasps my right hand, brings it to his nose, and inhales deeply.

My stomach bottoms out. *Oh no. Oh God.* I'd briefly stroked my pussy with that hand. My face grows hot.

What will he think?

A tingle races across my bottom cheeks.

Will he be angry? Will he punish me?

Visions of him yanking me over his knee to crack his palm across my ass leave me sweltering with need. Aroused. The prospect of him chastising me is causing my nipples to harden, my breaths to come faster, and the aching in my core to deepen.

"Little female, were you touching yourself?"

My mouth goes dry. "Yes," I whisper. "I'm sorry. Please forgive me. Please don't be angry." I nearly cringe at how pathetic I sound, but I can't bear the thought of him believing I'd just behaved indecently. I swallow hard as I await his response.

His eyes darken, and I'm not sure what to think. He drops my hand and leans closer. "Did you bring yourself to a climax?"

I shake my head. "No-no. I just felt around to see how sore I was this morning. I-I barely touched my clit. It was very fast and innocent, I swear it."

He throws the covers back and cups my pussy hard. I jolt against his possessive touch and soon find myself fighting the urge to hump his hand.

He loosens his hold and delves two digits into my core, sliding straight inside. I gasp at the abrupt fullness. His fingers are huge.

"I don't mind you touching yourself, Ellie, as long as you never lie to me about it. If I ask if you've pleasured yourself, I want an honest answer from you, even if it brings shame to your delicate human sensibilities. In fact, if you ever pleasure yourself in my absence, I want you to inform me immediately upon my return. Do you understand?"

I nod as the knot of worry coiling in my stomach unwinds. "Yes, of course. Thank you." I'm not sure if I'm thanking him for giving me permission to touch myself whenever I please, or if it's because I'm grateful he doesn't plan to punish me.

He tilts his head to the side, studying my expression as he continues pumping two thick fingers in and out of my slick center.

"Do you feel guilty?" he asks.

"Guilty?"

"For touching yourself." He withdraws from my core only to immediately swirl his thumb over my clit.

"I…" My voice trails off. He expects an answer. An honest one. I don't want to tell the truth, but I also don't want to risk getting caught in a lie. "Yes," I admit. "I feel guilty." I feel like I was caught doing something that's strictly forbidden, never mind that Tornn just gave me permission to touch myself.

He raises an eyebrow at me, appearing suddenly stern. "Would you like me to help you expunge that guilt, little female?"

"How would you do that?"

His eyes glitter for a moment, and he stares at me for so long that I start to think he doesn't plan to answer. Eventually, he says, "I could spank you to help alleviate your feelings of guilt," in a low rumbling tone that makes me quiver with longing.

My breath catches, and I struggle to find my voice. I hold his gaze as he continues stroking the most sensitive part of me. Fear and desire converge, causing deep aching pangs in my core. I'm close to climaxing. A few more caresses to my clit and surely I'll shatter…

But Tornn retracts his hand before I can reach the precipice of ecstasy. I whimper at the loss of his touch. He reaches underneath me and grasps my right cheek, giving it a hard squeeze. I gasp more from the surprise of his manhandling than from the pain. Only a faint sting lingers in the aftermath of yesterday's spanking.

"You don't need to punish me," I say in a beseeching tone. "I-I don't think a spanking could help release my guilt. Besides, I didn't really do anything wrong—you said it's okay if I touch myself. A spanking isn't necessary." I hold my breath, hoping he doesn't flip me onto my stomach and start swatting away at my bottom.

And yet… the idea of submitting to his authority sets my desires ablaze. The heat pulsing in my core strengthens, and my clit throbs so hard that it's all I can do to keep from reaching down and rubbing myself to a climax as he watches.

Surrender. I want to surrender to him, even if it hurts. Especially if it hurts. Because there's a sweetness to the pain that I crave beyond all reason.

"I think a few hard smacks to your bottom will do you some good," he says as he draws a hand down my inner thigh. His eyes meet mine. "In fact, I think you're aching for it, Ellie."

Chapter 12

TORNN

THERE IS NO QUESTION ABOUT IT—THE PROSPECT OF punishment excites my little human female. Her pink nether lips are gleaming under a sheen of arousal, and the intoxicating scent of her excitement hovers in the air.

She blushes as I guide her into a sitting position, and she lowers her head, trying to allow her long dark locks to shield her bosom. I quickly brush her hair over her shoulders, then reach for one nipple and pinch it until she whimpers.

"I want you to present yourself for chastisement, sweet human," I say, moving to her other nipple and giving it the same harsh treatment. I'm rewarded with another needy whimper.

"Present myself?"

"Yes. I want you to bend over the bed with your

bottom lifted high and your legs spread wide. I want an unhindered view of your soaking wet pussy as I spank you."

Her expression fills with shock, but she slowly climbs off the bed, and I watch with satisfaction as she assumes the ordered position. Such a good, obedient little female she is. My dual shafts harden, sticking straight up as I remain seated on the bed. She glances at my erections and her eyes widen.

Sliding off the bed, I circle around to stand behind her. Her legs are parted to give me a perfect view of her wet, swollen parts. I step closer and run a hand over her ass but don't find any marks from her previous spanking.

"The next time you experience guilt, sweet human," I say as I alternate massaging and squeezing her bottom cheeks, "all you must do is ask for help in atoning for your sins. I'll always give you what you need."

She whimpers and shuffles in place, her feet leaving the floor momentarily only for her to resume the original position. My cocks throb harder. I like watching her struggle to obey, especially when she surrenders in the end.

I press a hand to her lower back and deliver the first blow, letting my palm impact her cheeks with an echoing slap. She gasps and rises on her toes, but she doesn't try to evade the next smack, or the one after that.

I administer ten rapid spanks in total, just enough to make her bottom sting. She didn't disobey me, but for a reason I can't quite grasp, the idea of her carrying around guilt leaves me unsettled. Certainly a quick dose of punishment will help expunge the shame she harbors over touching her pussy.

My balls vibrate as I admire the slickness between her thighs. I help her stand, only to immediately lift her up and place her in the middle of the bed atop the disheveled covers. Before she can ask what I'm doing, I shove her thighs wide apart and bury my face in her sweetness.

Fluxx. The taste of her is celestial. I can't get enough of her feminine pungency. I drag my tongue up and down the seam of her nether lips, then settle my attentions on her distended clit. It's so swollen, it's protruding from her folds. I like that she's so responsive she can't hide her desires from me. I like that I know the instant she becomes aroused—I would have to be dead not to detect her excitement.

Her hands delve into my hair, tangling in my short locks. Recalling how she enjoyed the vibrations of my balls, I release a steady growl as I continue worshiping her button with my tongue.

It doesn't take long to make her shatter. She tightens her grip on my hair and cries out as her center jerks against my face. I pay homage to her clit until the last remnant of her release undulates through her and she goes limp.

I pull back and meet her gaze, then wipe my mouth on my arm. Part of me enjoys the fresh blush that covers her face. Some of my actions have scandalized her, and I cannot wait to see how she reacts when

I start training her bottom hole to accept my upper shaft.

"You're *fluxxing* delicious, Ellie."

Her blush deepens, but she doesn't respond. Her eyes dart around the room as she avoids my gaze. I lift her against the pillows, positioning her so she's sitting upright, then I angle my erect upper appendage toward her mouth.

"Open up, little female. I tasted you. It's your turn to taste me."

ELLIE

I stare at Tornn's upper cock as trepidation rushes through me. He's so huge, I'm not sure how I'll successfully take him in my mouth. But I must try. The urge to please him is overwhelming, and fresh waves of desire stir within me as I lick my lips and prepare to obey my strict alien husband.

I dart my tongue over a blue drop of his essence that clings to the tip of his shaft. To my surprise, he tastes… sweet. Like vanilla-frosted sugar cookies. My favorite dessert. I almost smile at the comparison but can't manage the movement because he's suddenly pressing his length further into my mouth.

He holds my face in his hands and peers at me with the most affectionate look he's given me yet.

"So nervous and shy in the bedroom," he says, "yet so willing to please."

Even if I didn't have my mouth filled with dick, I wouldn't know how to respond. I stare up at him, desperate for guidance. What the hell am I supposed to do now? I haven't the first clue, but relief flows through me when he takes the lead and starts moving his shaft in and out of my mouth.

As he thrusts inside, hitting the back of my throat, tears burn in my eyes, and I struggle not to gag. It doesn't hurt, and I can't claim I want him to stop, but it's not the most comfortable activity either. How long will he keep pounding my face?

With each rapid drive into my mouth, his vibrating balls hit my neck and chin. His semi-erect lower shaft, pushed to the side, drags along my cheek.

He tightens his grip on my jaw and drives faster and deeper. His feral growls reverberate off the walls.

Just when I think I can't take another rapid thrust, his appendage throbs in my mouth and he suddenly erupts, spurting his sugary essence across my tongue and down my throat.

He doesn't pull out of my mouth just yet, giving me no choice but to swallow, though it takes three huge gulps for me to accept all of his seed.

He withdraws his spent shaft and immediately replaces it with his now fully hard lower appendage, a wicked gleam in his dark, purple eyes. He strokes a hand through my hair as his balls vibrate steadily against me.

"Breathe through your nose," he orders, and he

doesn't start thrusting his second length into my mouth until I've successfully taken over a dozen deep breaths. "Good little female."

Good little female. I should be outraged when he says things like that, but I'm not. Instead, his oddly phrased but complimentary words fill me with warmth and make me want to do a good job of sucking his appendages.

He tightens his hold on my face and commences a steady drive in and out of my mouth. He lasts longer this time but eventually shoots his sugary essence down my throat, though I struggle to swallow all of it and a small amount trickles from the corner of my lips. He withdraws his shaft from my mouth and wipes at the blue liquid, gathering it on his finger, then he touches my lips, beckoning me to swallow every last drop.

He lays down beside me and gathers me close. I shyly snuggle into his embrace. His huge muscular arms surround me, and I rest my cheek against the glowing markings on his chest.

"How old are you?" I ask. A thousand questions about Tornn and his people speed through my mind, but for whatever reason, this one comes out first.

"By human standards, I am thirty-eight." He clears his throat. "How old are you, Ellie?"

"Twenty-one." I breathe deep of his masculine scent and try to work up the courage to ask my next question. "So, what's the average lifespan of a Darrvason?"

"Most Darrvasons reach the age of one hundred,

though there have been outliers who've seen one hundred and fifty years."

Relief crashes through me. We barely know one another, and I shouldn't be contemplating a future with him or worrying myself over whether he'll die decades before me or vice versa, but it would seem the average lifespans of our people match up. The oldest human on the *Jansonna* is almost one hundred and forty. Close enough.

Eventually, I withdraw slightly from Tornn's arms and trace the symbols on his chest. His breath catches and I swear the markings glow brighter, but surely I must be imagining it. I resist the urge to scratch my arms. No idea why, but they're suddenly itching again.

"I've never seen markings like these before," I say. "Are they tattoos of some kind?"

"They are my ancestral markings, and I was born with them. All Darrvason males are born with markings unique to their family. My forefathers were born with these very markings across their chests, and our sons will be born with identical markings as well."

"Only sons? Darrvason females aren't born with ancestral markings?"

A strange look enters his eyes, and he frowns. "I must leave soon and attend to some business on the ship," he says after a long moment, completely ignoring my question, "but I promise I'll return to you before the midday meal."

Chapter 13

TORNN

PADDAX BLINKS UP AT ME AS I FROWN AT HIS condition. His entire body is covered in huge red splotches, remnants of the unusual virus his mate injected him with. But he's awake and breathing, and the lead physician just finished assuring me that he would soon make a full recovery.

"Sheila," he gasps. "Where is she?"

"In the brig," I reply, then quickly add, "she has not been harmed."

He sighs and gives me a thankful nod. "She didn't want to do it," he says. "We were in bed, preparing to mate, when she suddenly gave me an apologetic look and told me she was sorry, though I didn't know what she was talking about until I felt the tingle of the hypospray on my neck."

"Captain Varll informed me as such," I reply,

"though he says Sheila is keeping quiet in the brig. She won't answer any questions. In fact, she hasn't uttered a single word since she was taken there."

Paddax reaches for a mug of water with a shaky hand. I wait patiently as he drinks and sets the mug aside. "I suspect someone on the *Jansonna* coerced my mate into harming me. A human—or perhaps a group of them—who don't want our alliance to succeed. If our scientists hadn't been quick to develop a vaccine, a deadly plague would've swept through the *Haxxal*."

"I agree." I glance around the medical bay, but no one is standing close enough to overhear our conversation. "Did your mate speak about her life aboard the *Jansonna* at all? Did she tell you anything about herself or her family? Anything about the job she had on the worldship?"

He shakes his head. "No, nothing. She didn't talk much but seemed very excited to mate, so I immediately took her to bed. I realize now her eagerness was a ploy to catch me off guard." His jaw tenses, and I can't help but wonder what Paddax will do with Sheila once she's returned to his custody.

"Doctor Lorzz says I'll be well enough to leave in approximately ten to fifteen days. I promise I'll personally question my mate and get answers from her. I'll make her confess every last secret she has." A look of resolve crosses his face.

"As you know, it's protocol for our security officers to question her multiple times a day while she's in the brig. That will continue, however if she remains uncooperative, I have faith that you'll be able to extract the answers we need."

Paddax grabs my arm. "No one touches her." His eyes flash with rage. "No one touches her but me. If I find out anyone caused her physical harm or threatened her, I will challenge them to *lahhkda*. She's mine to deal with. *Mine*." His eyes widen as he looks at his hand that's still clutching my arm. Then he quickly releases me and glances away.

"I give you my word that no harm will come to your female, Officer Paddax. Be well." I understand his anger and his possessiveness toward Sheila. If I were in his place, I would be furious with my mate but also eager to have her back in my keeping, where I could ensure her safety and also question her until she made a full confession.

It's in the best interest of my people to investigate the matter concerning Sheila in private without alerting Captain Warren or his command team. Just in case any of the *Jansonna's* leaders are involved. If they are, even all twelve Star Gods won't be able to save them from our wrath. My people won't take kindly to the alliance being broken.

I exit the medical bay and venture to the bridge, where the captain is waiting with the most recent report on the probes we'd deployed to investigate various planets of interest.

I stand at a scientific panel near the back of the bridge, scanning the report with a critical eye. One out of six planets we sent probes to investigate are suitable for humankind. Hope rises in my chest. The planet in question is sixty-eight percent water, has breathable air, and contains several large continents that are teeming with life.

"What do you think, Admiral?" Captain Varll asks with an eager gleam in his eyes.

"Alter course for Planet 58-Zallnanis," I say. "Inform the entire fleet." I continue to study the readings as the captain hurries off to follow my commands.

Indeed, 58-Z is perfect. I swipe through a series of images of the planet's surface and feel an instant wistfulness for the Darrvason homeworld. But our planet is gone. Destroyed by our greatest enemy.

As I examine the report further, I realize 58-Z is large enough to share. Could I convince Emperor Radakk and his advisors that we should settle on 58-Z with the humans rather than keep looking for a second habitable planet to call our own?

Many of the emperor's advisors have already spoken against sharing a planet with humankind—claiming it could lead to eventual war, particularly if the humans ever make significant advancements in their weapons technology—but an idea is already forming in my mind. An argument the emperor won't be able to ignore.

The longing to create a new home outside the confines of the *Haxxal* is so strong, I envision myself murdering any advisor who dares to speak against the idea of settling on 58-Z.

I transmit the data, including all the images of lush forests and fertile grassy lands, to Emperor

Radakk. He responds almost instantly, asking me to join him in his quarters.

There's a shudder as the *Haxxal* falls out of hyper-drive. I glance at the viewscreen and count the other ships in our fleet. Fourteen. Well, fifteen if the *Jansonna* is included. As I make my way off the bridge, I listen as Captain Varll continues barking orders and crew members rush to set a course for Planet 58-Z.

The lights in the corridor dim for a brief moment before I hear the familiar hum that indicates the *Haxxal* has just achieved hyperdrive. Six moon cycles. That's how long it'll take to reach 58-Z, assuming we don't run into any difficulties along the way. A growl rumbles from my throat when I remember the attack on Paddax.

I start to compile a mental list of urgent items as I approach the emperor's quarters. Later today, I will make a quick, surprise trip to the *Jansonna* to threaten Ellie's uncle and ensure the repugnant male leaves the families of the Darrvason brides alone. I'll take my personal shuttle for that meeting, and dark pleasure rolls through me as I imagine the captain's face when I threaten his life.

Strict boarding protocols must also be put in place before we take possession of the next wave of human females. And the alliance with the humans must be renegotiated, which means I'll have to meet with Captain Warren *and* his command team soon, though that meeting will need to be scheduled in advance. I must bring reinforcements to that meeting as well—the tallest, most fierce looking Darrvason security officers and advisors to better intimidate the captain and his pitiful command team.

Before I can add additional items to my list, a thunderous snarl echoes down the corridor I just passed.

My senses on high alert, I spin on my heel and run toward the sound of an enraged male. Just as I reach the corridor, a golden-haired human female bolts past me. Understanding dawns, and I don't make a move to touch her or stop her, though I don't resume my travels to the emperor's quarters just yet. If another male touches the golden-haired female—a male who isn't her mate—then *lahhkda* will likely be decreed and the corridors will fill with blood.

The woman's mate barrels around a corner and surges past me. He's only half-dressed, wearing a pair of black pants but nothing else. No shirt or boots. I don't recall his name but recognize him as a security officer who recently transferred to the *Haxxal* from one of the smaller ships in our fleet.

The male sprints faster and catches the female before anyone dares to touch her. He tosses her over his shoulder, turns around, and stalks in my direction, presumably taking his errant mate back to his quarters to face a reckoning. His eyes widen as he notices me for the first time, though his steps don't falter.

"Admiral," he says in a respectful tone, inclining his head briefly.

"Officer," I reply with a nod of my own.

He soon disappears down the corridor, and I resume my walk to Emperor Radakk's quarters, all the while resolving that I must continue filling Ellie with my seed multiple times a day. The thought of her running off and putting herself in danger... I growl at the prospect, and I almost feel sorry for her when I consider how sore she's going to be by the time I've finished pounding her tonight.

Chapter 14

ELLIE

I GLANCE UP FROM MY TABLET WHEN HEAVY FOOTSTEPS sound in the entryway. My stomach flips at the dark look in Tornn's eyes. When he meets my gaze, his nostrils flare and he emits an ominous growl that causes the hair on the back of my neck to stand up. It also causes warmth to quake between my thighs and my breaths to quicken.

He stalks toward me, and I rise from my spot on the sofa. As he comes closer, I back away a few steps. I can't help it. There's a primal hunger surrounding him that intimidates me.

Have I done something wrong? Is he angry at me?

I've spent most of today reading on my tablet, but I can't imagine why that would make him angry. If he expects me to do housework, he hasn't mentioned it. Besides, he has a servant android that he showed me this morning before he'd left. In fact, the android is currently busy in the kitchen wiping down the counters.

"Tornn?" I inhale a shaky breath and glance around his quarters in search of an escape route should I need one. But there's nowhere to run and nowhere to hide. I already know I'll never make it out of his quarters. The door won't open for me. And if I try to hide in a closet or under his bed, I have no doubt he'll be quick to pull me out—if I even manage to outrun him and make it there in the first place.

He backs me against the viewscreen and places his hands on either side of my head, then leans down and runs his nose along my neckline, taking deep inhales.

"I am going to pound you until you're sore between your thighs and dripping with my seed, little female." He nips at my ear, his sharp teeth scraping my flesh. Goosebumps rise all over my body, and a shiver rushes down my spine. Tension coils in my nether area, a heated *pulse pulse pulse* that causes my panties to feel damp.

Well. At least he's not mad at me. But my relief over this realization is short-lived because he abruptly grips the neckline of my shirt and rips it down the center, exposing my bosom. Though I'm wearing a bra, I instinctively move my hands to shield myself, but he smacks my hands away and snarls in my face, bearing his sharp, pointed teeth.

I drop my hands to my sides and take a deep breath. Tremors rack my body as my apprehension grows. Tornn might not be angry with me, but he could still hurt me during a rough session of copulation. I'd thought him rough last night and this morning, but there's an especially dark glimmer in his eyes that promises savagery.

He finishes tearing the remnants of my shirt off my body, then does the same with my bra and the loose pants I'm wearing. Oh, and my panties. Those get torn to pieces. A whimper leaves me as I watch him toss the shredded fabric to the floor. He presses me hard against the viewscreen, and the cool surface is a stark contrast to the heated pulsations between my quivering thighs.

Grasping my hair, he pulls me away from the viewscreen and pushes me to the floor on my hands and knees. The floor is hard and cold, but I don't dare make a move to get up. If he wants to pound me on the floor, I will cooperate. Besides, what choice do I have? If I resist, I have no doubt he'll punish me, and my bottom cheeks involuntarily clench as I remember the two spankings he's given me.

"Lift your bottom higher and part your thighs wider, little female," he says with a growl. "Show me the tight, wet hole I'm about to fuck."

His crass words cause my face to heat. I hurry to comply with his demands, and the cool air in his quarters wafts against my aching pussy as I spread myself to his liking.

As I stare straight ahead, facing the kitchen where the servant android is still busy wiping down the counters—how fucking dirty are they, anyway?—I hear the sounds of rustling fabric and boots being kicked off.

My pulse accelerates and warmth undulates in my center, my clit throbbing so hard that I find myself anticipating the vibration of his scrotum while he slams into me from behind.

I glance over my shoulder, eager for a look at Tornn in all his naked glory. I'm not disappointed. He stands above me like a conquering warrior, his textured muscles gleaming in the overhead lights, the ancestral markings across his chest glowing. Both his cocks are fully erect, sticking straight out with drops of his blue essence glistening on the bulbous tips. I can easily see that his balls are already vibrating, and my breath catches in my throat.

He releases another growl, and as he holds my gaze, he reaches down and fists his cocks, taking one in each hand. He kneels behind me on the floor, still pumping his shafts, and I turn back around and brace myself for the first hard thrust into my center.

He doesn't make me wait long. Before I take my next breath, he aligns one of his lengths—his lower one, I think—with my entrance and shoves inside with a feral roar that echoes off the walls.

Grasping my hips so hard I yelp, he sets an unhuman pace of pounding me, surging into my depths with so much force, he causes me to slide forward on the floor. His vibrating balls keep hitting my clit, and *oh God oh God oh fuck* it doesn't take long for me to shatter. I cry out in the throes of a sweeping climax.

For the next two hours, Tornn behaves as though he's possessed. He claims me again and again, spilling his seed inside me, only to withdraw his spent shaft and shove his other cock into my depths. He needs little more than a few seconds to recover in between mating sessions.

My knees and palms ache from the uncomfortable position on the floor, but he seems so lost in his fervent need for me that I'm not certain he would even hear me if I asked to change positions.

I lose count of the orgasms he gives me. I'm helpless to stop the quaking bliss from gripping me as his vibrating balls press against my throbbing clit.

When I no longer have the strength to remain upright and I collapse on the floor, he lifts me and positions me over the side of the sofa, though he does take a moment to place a pillow beneath my head before he enters me again. It's the only sign I have that he's still in there somewhere, that he hasn't gone totally mad with lust.

"You're mine, sweet human," he says as he slams into my aching pussy. "Mine."

Chapter 15

ELLIE

I watch in fascination as the servant android hangs Tornn's clothing next to mine in the huge closet. The remarkably lifelike android resembles a Darrvason male, though it's slightly shorter and less muscular than Tornn himself. It blinks every few seconds, and its chest rises and falls as though it's breathing, which I find a tad unnerving.

Most of the time, the android rests in a compartment in the wall near the entryway. But when there is cleaning to be done or laundry to be washed, it magically makes an appearance. It's a bit eerie when I'm putting dirty dishes in the cleaning receptacle and the android walks in, says something to me in Darrvason, and politely scoots me out of the way and takes over the task.

The android shuts the closet door and heads for

the bathroom, a bag of cleaning supplies in its hand. I peek into the spacious bathroom and watch as it withdraws a large blue object from the bag. It presses a button on the device and waves it over the bathroom mirror, removing the faint water splotches I'd carelessly left as I'd brushed my teeth and washed my face earlier.

I move away from the doorway and sink onto the bed, my mind whirling with the events of the past few days. I'm mated to a Darrvason male whose desires are far more ravenous than I would've ever imagined. Heat blossoms on my face and my core tightens with pleasure as I recall the long, hard pounding he'd given me last night. I squirm in place and feel the soreness between my thighs. For a reason I can't fathom, I experience a surge of satisfaction as the lingering ache resonates through my center.

After a while, a sense of restlessness hits me, and I peer around the tidy room. I'm not used to having idle time on my hands. It makes me feel guilty. Like I'm committing some terrible sin. On the *Jansonna*, I was always busy. Everyone was expected to contribute to the running of the ship. Those who slacked off faced severe consequences. Reduced rations, relocation to less desirable living quarters, and non-admittance to recreational rooms, to name a few.

Not that I haven't enjoyed the sudden downtime, during which I've taken countless bubble baths and reread several of my favorite history books, but there's an itch inside me that keeps growing. The need to be useful in some way.

With a frustrated sigh, I hop off the bed and trudge into the sitting area and pause in front of the huge viewscreen. Longing pangs in my chest when I glimpse the *Jansonna*. I miss my family and friends. My heart aches. I miss Nathan and the gentle love we'd shared.

A faint *beep beep beep* sounds in the background, intruding on my thoughts, and I turn and scan the room, wondering what the servant android is up to now. But the android is walking quietly toward its home in the entryway, its morning tasks complete, and the beeping is coming from much closer. The noise also sounds familiar… but there's no way it's what it sounds like.

My gaze falls to the reading tablet I'd left on an end table next to the long sofa. The screen isn't lit up, but as I step closer, I'm certain that's where the noise is coming from.

I pick the tablet up, sit down, and press a button to illuminate the screen. In the upper left corner, a text bubble appears. At first, I think it must be an old message—surely no one from the *Jansonna* would be able to contact me from this distance—until I notice the date and time.

Today. From a few seconds ago.

My pulse accelerates when I realize who it is, and my hands start trembling.

Nathan.

I swallow hard and glance toward the entryway, cold terror skittering through me as I imagine the fallout of Tornn catching me in a text conversation with my fiancé. Ex-fiancé. Whatever.

I've known Nathan my whole life, and I still have feelings for him. If not for the Darrvasons and the alliance, I would be going forward with my plans to marry him. In a couple of months, we would've been husband and wife. We'd planned to get married the week after my twenty-second birthday, on the day of our five-year anniversary.

It takes me several tries to open the text bubble because my hands are shaking so hard. But I finally manage to swipe it open, and my eyes scan the message.

Ellie,

If you're reading this, it means I was able to successfully amplify the signal on my personal comm and penetrate the Haxxal's *shields so I might send you a message. Rest assured that I'm using an encrypted but fluctuating comm number that should prove untraceable if the Darrvasons somehow detect it.*

I miss you and I'm heartbroken that you're gone. The Jansonna *isn't the same without you. I pray that no harm has come to you.*

Please write when you are safely able to do so.

Love,

Nathan

Tears blur my vision and my entire body trembles. Sometimes late at night when neither of us could sleep, Nathan and I would text one another. He'd rigged up a program from his personal desk comm in his quarters that had allowed him to send messages straight to my tablet.

All interpersonal communications on the *Jansonna* are strictly monitored, but the messages we'd shared had remained secret. Undetectable by any nosey morality or security officers.

We could talk innocently about our desire to get married and start a family without a morality officer suspecting we meant to have intercourse, and we could discuss our fears about the inept command team without fear of getting accused of mutiny.

I count the days since I left the *Jansonna*. Four days. Which means it's been five days since I've seen Nathan, since he hadn't come to the docking bay to see me off on the day I was handed over to the Darrvasons. On the day Tornn claimed me as his mate.

Only five days. Yet it feels like so much longer.

I glance at the entryway and my stomach flips. Tornn probably won't return for another two hours. Thus far, he's joined me for the midday meal every day since I've come to live with him.

After taking a deep breath, I type my reply to Nathan.

. . .

Nathan,

I'm so happy to hear from you. I miss you too. I promise I'm okay. Please don't worry. How are you doing and how are things going on the Jansonna? *Any update on the repairs to the worldship? How are my mother and sister faring?*

Love,
  Ellie

My stomach twists in a weird way when I type the word *love*, and I almost hesitate to send the message. But I tell myself I'm just overwhelmed by recent events and finally hit the 'send' button.

As I await Nathan's response, I can't help but feel a sense of unease. I won't lie—I'm petrified of Tornn finding out that I sent a message to Nathan. How would my possessive alien mate react? A shudder rushes through me as I imagine his dark purple eyes glittering with rage.

Maybe I should delete the text program from my tablet. Maybe I should just cut all ties with Nathan no matter how painful it is.

I peer around Tornn's spacious quarters, my gaze falling on the hallway that leads to his bedroom. This is my life now. The Darrvasons are going to considerable trouble to acquire human females from the *Jansonna*. I doubt Tornn would give me up under any circumstances—even if he found out I was talking to the human man I'd intended to marry.

The tablet starts beeping, and I'm quick to mute the volume.

It's a struggle not to cry as I read Nathan's response.

REPAIRS ARE GOING SO WELL ON THE SHIP THAT THE *command team has increased everyone's rations. We no longer have a water shortage either. Despite the improved conditions on the worldship, morale is low and there are constant whispers about plots to overthrow your uncle and his command team. The prospect of eventually losing one hundred more women followed by two thousand at the very end is daunting.*

I'm doing as well as I can, but it's my great hope that we'll see one another again someday. In fact, I know we will. Trust me on this.

Your mother and sister are carrying on as best they can. Your mother has resumed teaching already and your sister is helping her. Jenny requested a transfer from her duties in the recreational rooms to the education department, and I must admit I was surprised when your uncle approved it.

Speaking of the captain—he's being shadowed by a Darrvason security officer, and no one quite knows why. The Darrvason's name is Brute, and he rarely leaves the captain's side. He's a huge beast of an alien and he constantly glares at the captain as though he wants to kill him. It's unnerving but also amusing. It's rumored that the Darrvasons don't trust

Captain Warren to uphold his end of the alliance and that's why they've sent Officer Brute to watch him.

I hesitate to ask but I must. Have you been claimed by one of those vile Darrvason creatures yet? If so, what is his name?

MY MIND REELS AS I READ NATHAN'S MESSAGE THREE times. The news about my mother and sister pleases me, and the information about Officer Brute is also interesting. I can't help but wonder if Tornn is responsible for the Darrvason security officer shadowing my uncle. Perhaps Officer Brute is making sure Captain Warren doesn't harm the family and friends of the brides. My heart lifts at the realization that Tornn has likely already made good on his promise to protect my mother and sister.

But the last part of Nathan's message doesn't sit well with me. If I'm being honest, I'm annoyed that he just referred to Tornn as a *vile, Darrvason creature*. My fingers hover over the keyboard as I try to formulate a response.

I'm doing as well as I can, but it's my great hope that we'll see one another again someday. In fact, I know we will. Trust me on this.

Those three sentences bother me as well. What the hell is Nathan talking about? Warning bells go off in my head.

A shiver rushes through me and I again glance at the entryway. I swallow hard then focus on Nathan's message.

I don't want to tell him Tornn's name, and I'm

stunned when I search my feelings for the reason behind my reluctance. Though I've only known Tornn for four days and I didn't want to become his mate in the first place, I feel oddly protective of him. I worry revealing his identity to Nathan might put him in danger. Because the only way I will ever see my former fiancé again is if my people somehow betray the Darrvasons and break the alliance.

Shit shit shit.

What has Nathan gotten himself involved in?

I start typing.

Yes, I've been claimed by a Darrvason. His name isn't important.

What do you mean we'll see one another again one day? Nathan, what is going on? Don't be vague. Tell me exactly what you're talking about.

He doesn't respond for several minutes, so I go back through the history on my tablet and delete old messages, including today's messages, erasing all evidence of my illicit correspondence.

Finally, a new message flashes on the screen.

Forgive me, but I can't give you any details. Although my messages are encrypted, I cannot be too careful.

But I promise we'll be reunited one day. My only hope is that you aren't carrying one of those monster's babies inside you when that time comes. However, if you are pregnant when we're reunited, I'm friendly with a doctor who will take care of the situation for you.

My shift begins in ten minutes, and I must go.

I love you and I promise I'll message you again soon.

SICKNESS RISES IN MY THROAT. I DELETE HIS MOST recent message, not bothering to respond even to tell him good-bye.

What the fuck did I just read?

I run a hand through my hair and jump to my feet. As I pace in front of the viewscreen, I can't help but keep glancing at the *Jansonna*.

I place a hand on my stomach. What if I'm already pregnant but it's too early to know for certain? Tornn has ejaculated inside me countless times during the last few days. It might've already happened. It might be too late.

My heart aches. Not because I'm sad over the possibility that I might be carrying Tornn's child, but I'm heartbroken over Nathan's reaction to the prospect. His expectation that I have the pregnancy terminated leaves me both fuming and hurt. What if I'm carrying Tornn's child when I'm reunited with Nathan, and I want to keep the baby? Would he force me to get rid of the child? Would he leave me if I refused?

A dark thought strikes me. As possessive as Tornn is, I suspect the only way I would ever be reunited with Nathan is if Tornn is dead. My heart breaks at the prospect. I don't want any harm coming to the admiral, and I'm angry that Nathan is being so secretive.

The Darrvasons could've attacked the *Jansonna* and taken as many females as they wanted. They're that powerful. But they didn't attack us. Instead, they offered us an alliance. A trade. If all goes as planned, they'll lead us to a habitable planet and save humankind from perishing in the darkness of space.

Doubts and worries plague me, and it's a struggle to paste a smile on my face when Tornn finally returns for the midday meal.

But the moment the huge Darrvason envelops me in his arms and places a kiss atop my head, I melt and can't deny the warmth that pangs in my chest for him. If I'm being honest, I'm relieved to see him.

"Sweet human," he says into my ear, "what have you done in my absence?" He draws back to peer down at me, his hands resting upon my shoulders.

Act normal. Act fucking normal…

I gulp hard and gesture at my tablet. "Oh, just the usual. Read for a while. Also walked around your quarters looking for something to do, only for the android to thwart my every attempt at housekeeping. It wouldn't even allow me to place my own clothes in the closet." My face burns and I pray he doesn't detect my lies or the secrets I'm keeping.

My pulse spikes as I recall something ominous Tornn said on the day we first met, and it's all I can do to keep calm as his sternly spoken words resurface in my mind.

I also have no tolerance for lies. If you ever lie to me, sweet human, I won't hesitate to take a whip to your bottom. I'm your master, and you are not permitted to keep any secrets from me.

If I was truly loyal to Tornn, surely I would warn him that there was some nefarious plot afoot. But I fear his reaction if I tell him about my conversation with Nathan. How could I be certain he wouldn't hurt my former fiancé?

I think about the attack on Paddax and my worry deepens. What if Nathan had something to do with it? I suppress a shudder, not wanting Tornn to suspect anything is amiss. I press my face into his chest and mourn the loss of his closeness once he finally separates from me and guides me to the kitchen.

By some miracle, I manage to make it through the midday meal without arousing his suspicions.

Why do I feel so guilty? Surely I'm not developing feelings for the brutish male. It can't be that.

After we finish our meal, the servant android bustles in and starts clearing the table. I give it a dirty look and Tornn chuckles.

"You'll be thankful for the android's help with housekeeping when we have small children running around, sweet human." His eyes mist over with longing, and I suspect he's picturing the scene in his mind. My throat burns as I too suddenly imagine children running around his quarters or a cozy house on his homeworld.

"How many children do you want?" I find myself asking, even though it feels like a dangerous question.

The longing in his eyes gleams brighter, and a wistful smile tugs at his lips. "The emperor's advisors plan to encourage every newly mated couple to have as many children as they possibly can, in the interest of increasing our numbers more quickly. But I feel as though *four* is the perfect number. Perhaps the Star Gods will bless us with two sons and two daughters."

The lump in my throat thickens. "I've never asked you about how your people rear their children. Will I-I be involved in their upbringing? They won't be taken away and raised elsewhere, will they?" Why am I asking these questions now? The plot Nathan's involved in might very well succeed and then I would be ripped away from Tornn before we even had a chance to start a family.

Tornn reaches across the table and grasps my hand, and his expression turns gentle. "We will raise our children together, sweet human. I'm aware that some races raise their offspring in a communal manner, while others send their sons to a warrior camp as soon as they can walk, but that is not the Darrvason way. Our children will attend school for a portion of the day, and our sons will eventually enter an apprenticeship based on their natural talents, but they will reside in our home for years and years, likely until they reach adulthood at the age of nineteen."

I blink back tears. It sounds like Darrvasons rear their children in a manner similar to humans. And suddenly I'm furious at Nathan and I wish he'd never contacted me today. My feelings for him are so fucking conflicted right now I could scream.

Four days. I've only belonged to Tornn for four days and I'm already starting to question the life I'd thought I wanted with Nathan. Or maybe it's just Nathan that I'm questioning.

My only hope is that you aren't carrying one of those monster's babies inside you when that time comes. However, if you are pregnant when we're reunited, I'm friendly with a doctor who will take care of the situation for you.

As Nathan's texts play in my mind repeatedly, my anger toward him heightens. How dare he presume that I would want to get rid of Tornn's child? I think of my mother and sister and Tornn's promise to keep them safe from my uncle. I also think of my mate's promise to keep the other Darrvason brides safe.

I feel sick as I contemplate my conversation with Nathan. Though I haven't known Tornn for very long and I was forced to become his bride, the entire exchange with Nathan feels like a betrayal.

Tornn's deep longing to start a family is touching, and it makes him seem less forbidding. It *softens* him. It makes me want to get to know him better.

"Well," I finally say, "it's certainly a relief to know any children we have will remain with us."

Tornn opens his mouth to reply, but the doorbell abruptly rings and reverberates through his quarters. He glances toward the hallway, then rises to his feet. He helps me out of my chair and guides me to the sitting area in front of the viewscreen, and I try very hard not to glance at my tablet.

"I'll be right back, Ellie. Please wait here while I answer the door."

I sink down on the sofa and watch as he walks away, my mind in turmoil. If it weren't for Nathan, I could maybe allow myself to be happy right now. I could allow myself to be hopeful for an amicable relationship with Tornn and a future that involves raising a family together.

But I can't stop thinking about the good times I shared with Nathan, and I find myself making excuses for his horrible texts, particularly his comment about me carrying Tornn's baby.

Perhaps my former fiancé is under a great deal of stress. Perhaps he misses me so much that he's not thinking clearly and he's gone and gotten himself involved in a dangerous plot against the Darrvasons.

I hold my breath and listen as Tornn speaks with someone at the door. But they're talking in Darrvason and I can't understand a single word, and Tornn's huge body blocks whoever it is. He soon reaches forward and takes something from the visitor, and the door zips shut a second later when he steps back.

Carrying a large box, Tornn hastens in my direction, a pleased look in his dark purple eyes. He places the box on the sofa beside me with a flourish.

"A gift for you, my little female," he says in a warm voice.

"A gift? For me?" I ask rather stupidly, then blush as I peer down at the box.

"Open it."

I swallow hard, reach for the lid, and flip it open to reveal a stack of clothing in vibrant colors. I withdraw one of the garments and hold it up, allowing the fabric to billow downward as I gaze at the most beautiful dress I've ever seen. It's dark purple—nearly the same shade as Tornn's eyes—and the fabric shimmers in the overhead lights.

"Wow. Tornn, this is gorgeous. Thank you." I fold the dress, set it aside, and proceed to go through the remaining contents of the box.

There are five more dresses in a similar fashion to the first—long-sleeved flowing gowns that are surprisingly modest. At the bottom of the box, I find six pairs of cushioned slippers to match each dress. I'm stunned by his gift and more than a little embarrassed by the small wardrobe I'd brought with me—plain shirts and pants, many of them threadbare.

"These are all so lovely, Tornn. Thank you." I peer up at him with a smile.

"You are very welcome, Ellie. I am glad you like them." Just as he steps closer, his wrist comm beeps and buzzes, and he casts an annoyed look at the tiny screen. A sigh escapes him. "I must return to my duties, but I will be back later this evening."

Before I can ask if something's wrong, he turns on his heel and quickly marches out of his quarters, leaving me alone, surrounded by the beautiful dresses he'd just given me.

In the wake of his departure, I blink back tears as I gaze out the viewscreen at the *Jansonna*. If Tornn were the monster Nathan believed him to be, perhaps I wouldn't feel so conflicted, and perhaps I wouldn't feel so awful for keeping secrets from my mate.

I reach for my tablet, swipe open the text program, and type a message to Nathan even though I know it'll be hours before he sees it, as his shifts usually last ten hours.

HOW LONG? HOW LONG UNTIL WE'RE REUNITED?

I SEND THE MESSAGE AND HOPE I'LL HAVE AN ANSWER before the day is over. Nathan refused to give me any details about the plot against the Darrvasons, but maybe he'll give me a time frame.

After a glance toward the entryway, I delete the sent message from my tablet. We're conversing in Galactic Common instead of one of the older Earth tongues, which means if Tornn comes across the messages, he'll be able to read every word.

While I'm fluent in English and I can fumble my way through several other Earth languages, Nathan's parents, like many humans aboard the *Jansonna*, only spoke Galactic Common and thought allowing him to learn the old human tongues would've been a waste of time.

I set the tablet down and place all the dresses and shoes back into the large box. But before I can lift the box and carry it to the bedroom, the blasted servant android exits the kitchen and takes the box from my hands.

Chapter 16

ELLIE

AFTER A FULL WEEK SPENT IN TORNN'S QUARTERS, interacting with no one else but him, I find myself pacing in his absence, restless for a change of scenery. Frustration simmers anew inside me whenever I walk near the entrance of his quarters and the door doesn't open. Of course it doesn't. I ask him daily when I will be permitted to roam his ship freely, but he always says the same thing. *Not yet, sweet human.*

I've lost count of how many times we've copulated. How many times he's released his seed in my depths. Surely I'm covered in his scent enough that other males on the *Haxxal* won't be interested in me, though the idea of another male trying to claim me is more than a little distressing.

I'm used to keeping busy, and though I'm not the most extroverted person in the universe, I'm also used to interacting with lots of people every day. My students and their parents. Fellow teachers. My mother and sister and Nathan.

I sigh and run a hand through my hair.

The isolation is starting to get to me, but I don't think Tornn understands just how badly I need some freedom. Taking a deep breath, I resolve that I'll confront him once he returns to his quarters for the night. I pray he'll listen. I pray he'll at least give me a time frame. If I know exactly how many days I have left inside his quarters, it'll be helpful. I'll have something to look forward to. I'm tired of his vague answers and the way he always changes the subject—usually by distracting me with a long, intense mating session—whenever I ask him about the possibility of leaving his quarters and interacting with the other human females.

The door zips open and he strides beyond the entryway and into the sitting area where I'm currently pacing. I pause in my steps and brace myself for a confrontation. If he doesn't give in to my demands, I'm not sure I'll be able to remain calm.

His heated gaze roves over my body, and dammit I can't help but flush as warmth floods my center, anticipation swirling through me as graphic images of our most recent sexual encounters flit through my mind.

"My mate. I'm pleased you're still awake." He comes closer, and there's a cocky but predatory air about him that somehow serves to provoke my growing desires. It's suddenly too hot and I can't take in enough oxygen.

"I want to talk to you about something," I say, lifting my chin, trying to be brave. I place my trembling hands behind my back, clasping my fingers together so he doesn't notice my nervousness.

He finishes approaching and runs a hand down my arm, caressing one of the flowing, silky sleeves of the Darrvason-style dress I'm wearing. "You look beautiful in this gown, sweet human," he says as his eyes flash with pleasure. "The dark purple shade accentuates your already breathtaking features."

"Thank you," I force out, even though I'm agitated that he's doing it again. He's trying to change the subject. As though he's already guessed the subject I plan to broach and wants to distract me. Well, I resolve, as I lift my chin higher, it's not going to work this time. "Tornn, I want to discuss how soon I'll be permitted to leave your quarters. As many times as we've copulated during the last seven days, I'm confident that you've covered me in your scent, and I think it's safe for me to explore the *Haxxal*. I doubt any other males on your ship will bother me."

His face darkens and he grasps my chin. "*No*," he says. That's it. A one-word response uttered in an authoritative tone. No explanation. No promise about when I might be allowed some freedom.

"So, you basically lied to me, then?" I try to escape his hold, but he delves a hand into my hair, tightening his fingers in my locks and pulling me closer, nearly flush against his huge body. My neck aches as I stare up at his shocked expression.

"You're accusing me of being a liar?" His nostrils flare and his eyes flash.

"On the first day we met, I asked you if I was your prisoner. You said *no*, yet you haven't allowed me out of your quarters. The door won't open for me no matter how many times I walk up to it or how many buttons I press on the security panel on the wall nearby. Which means you purposely locked me in. It means you're keeping me as your prisoner."

As he peers into my eyes, he releases a low, steady growl that makes my stomach flip. "I informed you that you would be permitted to roam the *Haxxal* freely once you're adequately covered in my scent. Until that time, you must remain in my quarters where you will be safest."

"When?" I hiss. "When will that time come? You fuck me at least four or five times daily, Tornn. When will it be enough?"

"When I decide it's enough!" he answers in a booming roar that turns my insides to liquid. "I won't risk anyone harming you. I won't risk anyone attempting to take you from me. You're mine, Ellie. *Mine.*"

I blink against the burn of tears. "Please, Tornn." I try to keep my voice calm in a desperate attempt to salvage our evening. "I feel trapped and... well, I feel very trapped. *Suffocated.*" My pulse races. I almost say, 'I feel alone,' but stop myself in time. Admitting to my loneliness feels too personal. Tornn isn't a dear friend I can confide in. He's the arrogant alien who considers himself my lord and master.

His grip on my hair loosens, and he drops his hand from my chin. As he stares down at me, the glimmer of rage slowly fades from his eyes. He grasps my hand and laces his fingers through mine, then leads me to the sofa, beckoning me to sit next to him. Long moments pass as we sit in silence and gaze at the stars that streak by the viewscreen. We also have a clear view of several ships in the fleet, as well as the *Jansonna*, all the vessels traveling in the same hyper-space bubble.

He exhales slowly and though I'm not looking directly at him, I sense the tension draining from his body. Cautious hope flits through me. I hope he's going to see reason. I hope he's going to stop acting like a possessive barbarian. He can't keep me to himself forever. Not without causing me to drown.

He tightens his hold on my hand and I finally turn to chance a look into his eyes. To my relief, he no longer appears on the verge of a murderous rampage.

"I am uncertain how long it will take until I'm comfortable allowing you to roam the ship freely, Ellie, however, starting tomorrow I will take you on a daily walk through the corridors of the *Haxxal*. I recognize that you must remain healthy and fit enough to bear my offspring, and if you are feeling... *suffocated*, as you put it, I fear that could become a detriment to your health." He places a hand on my stomach. "How I long to see your stomach swell with our first child. There are times it's all I can think about."

I try not to allow a shadow to cross my face, but it isn't easy. He's finally going to let me out of his quarters, but he's only doing so because he wants to keep me mentally fit enough to bear his children.

Breeding purposes.

My uncle's taunting words echo in my mind. But Tornn is staring at me with an expectant look—he's waiting for my response. No doubt waiting for me to thank him for his generous offer to accompany me on daily walks throughout the corridors of the *Haxxal.* He's letting me out, but he's keeping me on a tight leash.

"Thank you, Tornn," I finally manage, though the words taste bitter.

"Growing up in my village," he says, "I witnessed many battles to the death take place over a female. A newly mated male would be confident that he'd coated his new bride in his scent, only for the female to get captured when she ventured off into the village without his protection. My mother's younger sister was stolen by a male from the mountains who was a stranger to our village. Her mate challenged the stranger to *lahhkda*—a battle to the death—and while her mate won, before he was able to decapitate the stranger and rescue my aunt, the stranger had already rutted her several times. He'd beaten her for resisting and taken her by force."

A chill rushes down my spine. I swallow hard, my mouth suddenly parched. I'm not in love with Tornn. I wouldn't be heartbroken if I were abruptly ripped away from him (that's what I tell myself, anyway) but I sure as hell don't want to be stolen away and violated by another male.

I spend a few moments processing all he's just told me. Eventually, I say, "I will admit, Tornn, that I believed your refusal to let me leave your quarters alone was an overreaction. That you were being a bit too high-handed, too possessive." I release a quaking sigh as goosebumps prickle my arms. "I am sorry for what happened to your aunt."

I want to ask how long until it'll be safe for me to leave his quarters without his company, but I can't quite work up the nerve to demand an estimate. Not after the story he just told.

He cups my face, his touch achingly gentle compared to a few moments ago when he'd clasped my chin and nearly yanked my hair. His eyes resonate with warmth tempered with resolve. "And I will admit, sweet human, that I feel violently possessive of you. I will also admit that I will likely keep you sequestered in my quarters for much longer than necessary. But I will not risk any harm coming to you. I am confident I would beat any male on the *Haxxal* who tried to steal you. I would win *lahhkda*. However, the thought of that male hurting you and rutting you before I reached you…" His voice trails off and he drops his hands from my face. He turns toward the viewscreen and exhales a shaky breath. His hands curl into fists at his sides and his entire body tenses. "It is a maddening thought."

Gradually, the tension leaves his body again. He slides closer and drapes an arm around my shoulders, pulling me close. My mind whirls as I try to process our conversation. Maybe my initial belief that he was overreacting and being too protective holds merit, but the story about his mother's sister is downright horrifying. Are his people truly so brutish? Isn't there any law and order among them?

"Tornn, how do young, unmated Darrvosan females stay safe in your culture? Are they kept behind locked doors until they come of age?"

His eyes flicker to mine as he gently rubs a hand up and down my arm. "A Darrvason female reaches maturity at the age of nineteen," he says, "and shortly before her nineteenth birthday, she is relocated to a safe, locked room in her family's home. As soon as she experiences her first heat, she's given to her mate—a male of her father's choosing—and then the male takes her to his home where they are expected to copulate until she's drenched in his scent."

"First heat?"

He nods. "It refers to the time she becomes sexually receptive. Her pussy swells and becomes wet, sometimes she develops a fever, and she is eager to be claimed by her mate. It also means she's ready to carry her first child." His gaze flits over my body, and I feel my nipples tighten within the confines of my bra. "From what I understand, human females do not experience heat in the way a Darrvason female does, but you still become wet and achy when you're eager to be mated."

His explanation causes my face to grow warm, and I'm very aware of his nearness. His thigh is pressed to mine, and his arm tightens around me. "Oh," I finally reply. "I had no idea."

Well, I sure have learned a lot about Darrvason mating practices this evening. My heart races when Tornn leans down and his warm breath puffs against my face.

I think he's going to kiss me. I think he's going to push me down on the sofa and have his way with me, and God how I'm aching for it.

If I'm this achy and hot with the wanting of him, I can't even imagine how a poor Darrvason female must feel as she's experiencing her first heat.

But he doesn't kiss me or maul me on the sofa. Instead, he draws back, rises to his feet, and nods to an empty corner in the room. "Come with me, Ellie, there's something I want to show you."

Chapter 17

TORNN

I HADN'T MEANT TO FRIGHTEN ELLIE WITH THE STORY about my mother's sister, but I need her to comprehend the full magnitude of the danger she might face if she leaves my quarters too soon. The *Haxxal* is a large ship, and my duties take me all over the massive vessel. Furthermore, I occasionally take a shuttle to other ships in the Darrvason fleet, and the idea of another male stealing her while I'm not even aboard the *Haxxal* is horrifying indeed.

I won't risk her safety. But her admission that she's *suffocating* in my quarters doesn't sit well with me. If I'm being honest, I'm offended that my company isn't enough for her. Brushing this thought aside, I open a hidden panel in the corner of the sitting room and turn to Ellie.

"This is a holo," I explain with a nod at the

hundreds of glowing symbols that adorn the inside of the panel. "Perhaps using some of the programs will help you feel... less suffocated. Here, let me show you. This is my favorite program." I press the twenty-sixth symbol and my entire quarters transform into a majestic, lush forest.

Ellie gasps and clutches my arm, her eyes going wide as she peers around the room. "Tornn. Oh, Tornn. Is this a forest from your homeworld?"

"No," I reply quickly, hoping she doesn't ask any further questions about Darrva. "This is a forest from the Brorrualan homeworld. It was my mother's favorite planet to visit. One of her brothers was an emissary to Brorrual so my family was permitted to travel freely there." I try to push away the darkness that gathers as childhood memories resurface. Everything changed with the destruction of my homeworld and the ensuing war against the Yelltzins.

"It's beautiful," she says in a voice filled with awe. She turns to me with tears gleaming in her eyes. "We don't have anything like this on the *Jansonna*. We have old, virtual reality headsets in our recreation rooms, but they don't come close to this." She strides to a nearby tree and reaches out slowly, as though expecting she truly might touch a physical object, then allows her hand to pass through the holographic projection.

I move to the panel and press another button, and suddenly we're standing on the balcony of a Friannaxan café that overlooks a majestic alien city which features some of the most beautiful architecture in the known universe. The murmur of conversation surrounds us as the aliens who call the city home sit at crowded tables speaking to one another while enjoying steaming cups of tea.

I grasp Ellie's hands and draw her closer. "Perhaps when you are feeling suffocated and I'm not around to take you on a walk, you can use the holo. I know you can't read the symbols, but you can test them all and figure out which are your favorites. Several years ago, we purchased this program from a famous Erusstian explorer named Rirra. He has visited hundreds of planets and created corresponding holo programs that project nature and city scenes based on real places."

A strange, unexpected warmth flows through me when Ellie gives me a wide smile and her eyes dance with joy. "This is marvelous, Tornn. Thank you for showing me this."

"You are welcome to use the holo whenever you wish, sweet human. I hope you will enjoy it."

Her face still bright with happiness, she eyes the symbols on the panel, and I sense her excitement to test every program. I hope the recreational activity will bring her a sense of calm the next time she feels restless. I still remember the agonized screams of my aunt's mate when he suddenly realized she'd gone missing. I also recall the bloody battle that took place in the streets after he challenged the stranger to *lahhkda*. And for as long as I live, I'll never forget the bruises I glimpsed on my aunt's body as her mate carried her home.

I remind myself that Ellie comes from a culture

that's vastly different from my own. While I'm not an expert on humans, I'm coming to understand that human females are granted freedoms that Darrvason females simply cannot have. Though human women don't go into heat, they still smell so *fluxxing* delicious that an unmated male might be tempted to claim one who's not thoroughly coated in her husband's scent.

Ellie's scent is sweet. When I first saw her on the *Jansonna's* docking bay, her beauty caught my attention first, but then a moment later her sweet, delectable scent had me so ensnared that I'd struggled to speak. Sweet human. That's why I call her that. Because she's so *fluxxing* sweet I could spend my entire day licking her all over and thrusting deep into her slick pussy until she's sore and dripping with my seed.

I know she wants a specific answer about when I'll allow her to freely roam the *Haxxal*, but I hesitate to give her a date or announce a certain number of days. Because I don't trust that I'll be able to keep such a promise. Until I'd claimed a mate of my own, I hadn't realized how intense the need to keep my female safe would be. If she never asked to leave my quarters, I might keep her here forever.

But we'll have children together one day. Hopefully soon. And our children will need to attend school and an eventual apprenticeship once their natural talents are identified. Until our children reach a certain age, Ellie will need to accompany them to school and various recreational and social activities. Logically, I know I must allow her to leave my quarters without my company in the near future.

Reaching for the panel, I press the very last symbol, and my quarters transform to a snowy mountaintop on Rurnnal Prime during a shimmering meteor shower. I draw Ellie closer, and she laces her arms around my waist. I try to remember if she's ever hugged me before, but I don't think she has. Not like this.

I hunger to claim her. My cocks are throbbing, my scrotum nearly at a full vibration. Yet I'm hesitant to leave this most satisfying embrace. I wrap my arms around her, holding her tight as the meteors blaze down upon the snowy, mountainous landscape.

Chapter 18

ELLIE

Tᴏʀɴɴ ᴄʟᴜᴛᴄʜᴇѕ ᴍʏ ʜᴀɴᴅ ᴀѕ ᴡᴇ ᴛʀᴀᴠᴇʀѕᴇ ᴛʜᴇ corridors of the *Haxxal*. It's the third day in a row that he's taken me on a walk, though like the previous days, we rarely pass anyone in the corridors.

"I thought thousands of Darrvasons called this ship home," I say as we round a corner and travel down yet another empty corridor. "Where is everyone?"

"These are the royal corridors of the *Haxxal*, passageways that were originally intended for the emperor's use only. After Emperor Radakk's great-great grandfather was repeatedly targeted for assassination, he ordered the *Haxxal* to be constructed with corridors that were solely for his use. Emperor Radakk, however, has granted the use of his royal corridors to a small number of trusted officers, crew members, and advisors."

Mild annoyance fills me and it's a struggle not to yank my hand from Tornn's grasp and give him a dirty look. He'd promised to take me on daily walks outside his corridor, but the virtually empty royal corridors feel like a loophole. But I quickly remind myself that this is a good first step in gaining more freedom, and perhaps in a few weeks he'll permit me the free roam I've been longing for.

I clear my throat. "Has anyone ever attempted to assassinate Admiral Radakk?"

"Only once. An advisor who held a grudge against the emperor attacked him on the bridge one day in full view of our highest-ranking officers. Before anyone could intervene, Emperor Radakk snapped the disloyal advisor's neck."

Thalia. I suddenly think of her and wonder how she's faring. I hope the neck-snapping emperor isn't being a complete monster to her. If only I could speak with her... I stifle a sigh. I would like to speak with the other human women too, but according to Tornn, none of them have been permitted to leave their respective mate's quarters yet.

I think my mate is over-the-top possessive, but it would seem many of his comrades are worse.

Tornn guides me down another corridor, and I'm surprised to see two males headed our way. They pause briefly and say, "*Kreullsha*," which I recently learned means *Admiral* in Darrvason. They each give a faint nod before rushing past us. Not for the first time since we'd started taking daily walks, I'm miffed that the passersby completely failed to acknowledge my existence.

"Why won't they talk to me?" I ask. "Whenever we pass a male in the corridor, they won't even look me in the eye, let alone greet me. And why won't you introduce me to any of them? If I'm to spend my life among your people, I think I should start learning names and at least…" My voice trails off when he shoots me a scandalized look.

He slows his steps and emits a low growl. "It would not be proper for unmated males to speak with you this early in our mating union. To talk to you or look you in the eye would be considered a great sign of disrespect to both of us. By ignoring you, they have shown that they have no intention of taking what belongs to me."

"So, when exactly will they start to acknowledge me?" I've never considered myself attention seeking, but being ignored is a shitty feeling, even though apparently the males hadn't meant to cause any offense.

"Unmated males must wait for an invitation to acknowledge a female who belongs to another male. The invitation must come from me, and it's tradition for three moon cycles to pass before an invitation is issued." He squeezes my hand and resumes his normal pace, and I gladly match his steps.

"An invitation? How does that work exactly?"

"An introduction serves as an invitation," he explains. "Once I greet them and tell them your name, they will be free to acknowledge you in passing and even hold short, respectful conversations with you as long as I am nearby."

"Three moon cycles?" I suppress the dramatic huff that really wants to escape my lips. "Where I come from, it's considered rude not to greet someone you pass in the corridors—male or female—unless of course the corridor is super crowded, then it's not expected at all, unless you see a person you consider a dear friend. What if *I* were to say 'hello' to the males next time we pass them in the corridors and initiate a conversation? Cultural differences aside, it might be nice to—"

His sudden growl cuts me off. As we near a familiar corridor that I'm pretty sure leads back to his quarters, he growls again and tightens his grip on my hand. "No. We will hold to tradition. Furthermore, you will refrain from blatant acts of disobedience, little female, or suffer my wrath." He aims a particularly stern glare my way.

A tingle races across my bottom cheeks, and heat simultaneously ignites in my core. Dammit. Why do his threats of punishment never fail to excite me?

Perhaps it's his extra deep voice that rumbles through me whenever he's being high-handed, or maybe it's the way his purple eyes glimmer as he gives me a scolding look.

When Tornn's nostrils flare and he takes a sudden, rapid inhale, I curse my traitorous body as well as his heightened senses.

He guides me into his quarters and the door zips

shut behind us. My stomach flutters when he pins me against the wall and lowers his face, looking me directly in the eye.

Anticipation curls through my insides, and steady pulses of warmth affect my center. I press my thighs tightly together, attempting to assuage the growing ache while also hoping to hide the scent of my building arousal. My heart pounds faster.

"Females are not supposed to question their mates," he says in an overly exasperated tone. "Females are supposed to obey without question and trust that their mate knows what's best for them." He clutches my upper arms and I think he wants to shake me. But he closes his eyes, takes a deep breath, then exhales slowly and refrains from getting rough with me. "You vex me, Ellie."

"Maybe you ought to return me for an alternate."

He tightens his grip on me. "*No.*" He snarls. "Even if my people didn't mate for life, I could not fathom returning you. I could not fathom being parted from you for a single day."

Before I draw my next breath, he grasps my face and kisses me soundly, sweeping his tongue into my mouth with a feral growl that sends heated tingles straight to my clit.

I shudder against him and run my hands along his sculpted chest as he deepens the kiss.

The blissful ache between my thighs grows stronger, and I undulate my hips, hoping to press my center against his, but with him bent down so far to kiss me, it's just not possible for our bodies to line up that way.

He pulls back and releases a dark chuckle, then tosses the fabric of my skirt upward and reaches up my gown. He cups my pussy and gives it a firm squeeze.

"Sweet, unruly little female." He kisses me again.

Chapter 19

TORNN

Not long ago, I'd believed if I rutted Ellie once, perhaps twice, that would be enough to cure my intense need for her. But I was wrong. So *fluxxing* wrong.

As I press her to the wall in the entryway and kiss her soundly with my hand wedged between her thighs cupping her warm little pussy, my need for her burns through my veins, more intense than ever before.

No matter how many times I claim her pussy or fuck her mouth, it's not enough. It's never enough. I want more.

Since I first met her, not a day has passed that my ancestral markings haven't tingled or itched in her presence. Sometimes when our bodies are joined together, other times while I'm holding her in my arms or just looking at her.

My need for her is maddening.

Our teeth clash as I deepen the kiss, growling as I squeeze her pussy harder and tangle my tongue with hers. Urgent whimpers drift from her throat, calling up my most primal desires.

I savor the scent of her sweet but pungent excitement. She's wearing panties but I can feel the wetness of her arousal soaking through the thin material.

With a quick movement, I tear the panties off her body and toss the remnants of fabric aside. Her gown comes next, though I'm careful to remove it without ripping it since I know it's one of her favorites. I leave it on the floor and scoop her up in my arms. As I carry her toward the bedroom, her slippers come off her feet, falling to the floor with a soft thud.

I place her on the bed and give her a stern look. "Stay there, little female. If you move off the bed, I'll take a strap to your bottom."

Her eyes widen, her breath catches in her throat, and the scent of her arousal heightens in the air. But as I back away, she remains in place on the bed, my sweet, obedient bride.

I hurry to the closet where I search for an old shirt I no longer wear. I tear a long, thick strip of fabric off, then hurry back to my mate's side. She's right where I left her, seated on the bed, her face flushed as she peers at the fabric I'm holding.

"Bend over the bed, Ellie."

She gulps hard and slides off the bed. As she gets into position, my cocks thicken further when I glimpse the moisture that's gleaming on her inner thighs.

"Good little female. Now, give me your hands."

She whimpers, no doubt realizing my intent to restrain her, but she quickly reaches back and offers me her hands. Small tremors affect her body, and her hands shake as I gather her wrists at the small of her back.

Using an intricate knot she'll never be able to unfasten, I tie her wrists together. Then I grasp her hips and hoist her higher on the bed, not stopping until her feet dangle above the floor.

I strip my clothing off and lean over her, growling at the feel of her naked body against mine. My erect shafts press upon her bottom as I place my lips at her ear.

"You're completely at my mercy, Ellie, and I'm going to pound you until your tight little pussy is sore and dripping with my seed, and there's nothing you can do about it. You have no choice but to lie here and take my cocks over and over again."

She trembles harder and emits another enticing whimper. The scent of her arousal keeps increasing, and when I drag my upper shaft through the seam of her folds, her center jerks slightly, the only movement she's able to make.

I straighten and grasp her bottom cheeks, pulling them wide apart, revealing her glistening pink nether lips and her adorable pucker. I make a mental note to replicate a set of plugs soon. Just the prospect of sliding into both her holes at the same time causes my cocks to lurch and my balls to vibrate faster.

With a primal snarl, I shove my lower shaft into

her, pump twice, then withdraw only to thrust my upper cock into her tight, wet center. She gasps and struggles against the restraints, and her feet kick briefly, slamming into my legs.

A dark chuckle escapes me, and I continue in this pattern, fucking her with one shaft for several strokes, then withdrawing only to immediately shove my other length into her. With each rapid drive, I make sure my vibrating scrotum impacts her swollen clit.

By the time she gasps through her third climax, my own release is rushing close, a twinge of sensation that starts at the base of my spine as my balls tense and both my cocks erupt in unison. As my lower shaft spurts into her depths, I fist my upper cock and send torrents of blue seed onto her back.

After I withdraw from her pussy and step away, I admire the sight of her prone on the bed, her wrists tied together, her back and arms covered in a thick layer of my essence. I lean over her and grasp her hair, giving it a harsh tug.

She moans and whimpers and the delightful noises coming from her tiny throat make me want to ravish her again.

So, I do.

My wrist comm keeps buzzing and beeping, and I know I'm needed elsewhere on the *Haxxal*, but *fluxx* I must have Ellie at least one more time.

I take her again and again, until it's late in the afternoon and I have no choice but to return to my duties or risk my comrades coming to look for me.

Before I leave my sweet human, I untie her wrists

and allow her to turn over on the bed. She blushes as her thighs rub together, her flesh sticky with her own arousal and my seed. She glances toward the bathroom, but I grasp her chin and wait until she meets my eyes.

"No cleaning up yet, little female," I say. "When I return for the night, I want to find you still covered in my seed. If you clean up even a small amount in my absence, I will punish you severely. Do you understand?"

Her face goes white, but she soon nods. "Yes, I-I understand."

"Good." I lean down to kiss her forehead. "I will return as soon as I can. You may put a robe on if you get cold, but absolutely no cleaning up. I want you to feel the stickiness of my seed covering you for the rest of the day—a reminder that you *fluxxing* belong to me and no other."

Chapter 20

ELLIE

I flush as I squirm on the sofa, my pussy sore from the hard pounding Tornn just gave me. He's been gone for about an hour, and I'm still shocked that he forbade me from cleaning up.

I'm wearing an oversized robe I found in his closet. It's soft and comfortable, but the fabric keeps sticking to my back, my arms, and my legs. I glance at the clock, hoping he returns sooner than expected. Will he allow me to bathe once he returns? Or will he claim me again and cover me in more of his seed before he eventually allows me to clean up?

As I look around the room, my gaze falls on my tablet, and a sense of unease spreads through me. *Nathan.* Is there a message waiting for me? Guilt flows through me and not for the first time, I consider deleting the texting program from the device.

Doesn't he realize how powerful the Darrvasons are? I can't fathom anyone on the *Jansonna* coming up with a plan to defeat the aliens. Tornn recently told me about the virus contained in the hypospray and how it failed, and I'm certain the Darrvasons will make sure the next group of human women don't bring any contraband aboard their vessels.

The *Jansonna* has a few missiles left in its arsenal, but from what Nathan has told me, it sounds like all the Darrvason vessels possess high-tech shields. And even if the *Jansonna* managed to strike and incapacitate one of the alien ships, other vessels in the Darrvason fleet would be quick to retaliate. All those aboard the worldship would meet a swift but brutal end.

More and more, I find myself hoping Nathan's insistence that we'll see one another again one day is nothing but foolish talk. That maybe he's only vaguely aware of a plot or two against the Darrvasons that will never actually get off the ground—like the many whispers about overthrowing my uncle and the handful of disorganized attempts to usurp his command.

I sigh and turn on my tablet, frowning at the screen when I see a message is in fact waiting for me.

Ellie, I'm sorry that I can't give you a time frame or any details. You need to stop asking. Just trust me. You still trust me, don't you?

. . .

I stare at his latest message, unsure of how to respond.

Tornn's handsome face keeps appearing in my mind, and it's impossible to stop thinking about him when my pussy aches from his claiming and his seed is drying on my skin.

I can't imagine sharing the same sexual activities that Tornn and I have enjoyed with my former fiancé. I can't even imagine kissing Nathan again. Is it possible we only shared a deep friendship that I mistook for love?

My feelings for Nathan aside, I want my mother and sister to remain unharmed. I want them safely settled on a planet. If someone from the *Jansonna* attacks the Darrvasons, the entire alliance might be jeopardized. The Darrvasons foiled the virus, but what if the next attack kills a few of the aliens? I doubt Tornn's people would turn the other cheek. Without a doubt, I know they would retaliate.

I finally type a reply.

You need to listen to me, Nathan. Whatever you're doing, STOP IT. No more plotting against the Darrvasons. It's not worth it, and you'll never succeed.

I want my mother, sister, and friends safely settled on a planet where they can start new lives. If the alliance is broken, that might never happen.

Darrvasons mate for life, and none of the thirty alien males who have already claimed human women will stand by and allow their mating unions to be threatened. Darrvason males are possessive and will stop at nothing to protect their mates.

Please reconsider what you're doing. Please give up your hope of seeing me again. I'm not yours anymore, Nathan.

Please do whatever you can to convince your accomplices to honor the alliance.

I SWALLOW HARD AND STARE AT THE REPLY I JUST typed, my finger hovering over the *send* button. Nathan isn't going to like my response, though his opinion doesn't really bother me. That's not why I'm hesitating to press *send*. I'm hesitating because he's my final link to the *Jansonna* and its occupants.

The final link to my mother and sister.

He hasn't yet invited them to his quarters so they might use his personal comm and speak with me—he keeps making excuses whenever I ask—but he at least provides me with daily updates about how they're doing.

But I remind myself that my mother and sister's safety is more important than the possibility of speaking with them again, and I finally press *send*.

Nathan's response flashes on the screen a few minutes later, and his words gut me. Okay, maybe his opinion still matters to me somewhat.

IT SOUNDS LIKE YOU'RE SIDING WITH THE DARRVASONS. *Which means you're a traitor to your people, Ellie.*

Do you like spreading your legs and being rutted like an animal by your alien mate?

What is your mate's name? I've asked you several times, yet you won't tell me. I think you're trying to protect him.

Traitor. Whore.

TEARS BURN IN MY EYES, BUT I BLINK RAPIDLY, refusing to cry over Nathan's cruel response. How dare he? The desire to maintain the alliance doesn't make me a traitor. It makes me fucking practical.

I delete our most recent conversation, turn the tablet off, and set it aside. I've never seen this side of Nathan before, but holy shit what a dick.

Tornn's gotten upset with me a few times, but he's never called me a hurtful name. He's never talked down to me in the same way Nathan just did.

I stare out the viewscreen at the *Jansonna*, my mind reeling as I try to figure out a way out of this mess. I could delete the texting program and hope for the best. Or I could confess what I know to Tornn.

Cold fear drenches me when I imagine telling my mate about the text conversations and a possible plot against his people. Would he punish me for keeping secrets? Would he ever trust me again?

But giving Nathan's name to Tornn is basically sentencing Nathan to death. If the Darrvasons don't kill him, surely my uncle will have him publicly executed for his treachery. While Nathan hasn't given me any real details about his plans, he did inform me that Captain Warren and his entire command team aren't involved in any way.

Besides, I know my uncle well enough to realize how desperately he wants the alliance to succeed. He wants the glory of being remembered as the last captain of the *Jansonna*. The captain who victoriously saw humankind settled on a new planet. He wants to be remembered as a *savior*.

Before I can decide what to do, Tornn returns to his quarters—hours earlier than expected. I rise from the sofa and face him, and my heart races when he gives me an affectionate look.

"Sweet human." He stands in front of me, his eyes roving over the robe I'm wearing.

"Tornn." My face heats when he steps closer and opens the front of my robe. "Are you back for the evening?"

"Yes." A pleased growl rumbles from his chest as he pushes the robe completely off me and peers at my naked body, looking at the sticky sheen of blue that covers my thighs and arms.

He walks around me to peer at my back, where the largest amount of his dried seed remains. Little tremors besiege me as he takes his time inspecting me, and I hold my breath, praying he doesn't think I tried to wipe any of his seed off.

"I like seeing you covered in my essence, Ellie, and I'm pleased that you obeyed me." He circles around to loom over me and places a finger beneath my chin, forcing my gaze to his. "Come. I'll give you a thorough bath, then we can enjoy a leisurely dinner together.

We can put one of the holo programs on while we eat and pretend we're millions of light years away from here. We can pretend we're on a beautiful planet. Just the two of us."

My throat burns. Tornn has no idea that my heart is in turmoil right now, no idea about the conversation I just had with Nathan. But a distraction is just what I need right now, and that's what he's offering me. He's also offering me companionship and gentleness, and my lonely soul latches onto his offer like it's my salvation.

"That sounds wonderful," I finally reply, offering my mate a small smile. I push away thoughts of Nathan and his stupid plot, vowing to enjoy what's left of the evening with Tornn.

Chapter 21

ELLIE

EVEN AFTER TWO WEEKS ABOARD THE *HAXXAL*, I'M still not used to mealtimes with Tornn. Or rather, I'm perpetually shocked by the food he consumes.

His diet seems to be seventy-five percent raw meat, and I shudder to think about where the meat comes from. He replicates various rice, bean, and vegetable dishes for us to share, but there's a refrigerator in the kitchen that is kept stocked with fresh slabs of meat, which are typically delivered in the evening.

I watch as he stabs a huge fork into the bloody pink meat on his plate and brings the whole thing to his mouth. With his razor-sharp teeth, he easily takes a bite. When a trickle of blood runs down his chin, he's quick to dab it away with a napkin.

"Would you like to try some?" he asks, nodding at

the platter of meat in the center of the table. "It's delicious."

"No, thank you," I say, gathering a forkful of steamed vegetables. "I've never eaten meat before and I'm not sure it would agree with me." I don't want to tell him I think it looks gross. We're still getting to know one another, and I don't want to cause any offense.

He glances at the food replicator. "Our engineers are currently working on programming our food replicators to produce more human foods. We had cooks from the *Jansonna* send us samples of popular human cuisine, and I believe you'll have more choices in a few days."

"Wow, Tornn, that sounds really nice. Thank you." My spirits lift. Every now and then he does or says something that gives me hope. Hope that the Darrvasons aren't coldblooded savages who consider females their property.

I still haven't had the opportunity to speak with any of the other human brides, but I hope they're all faring well with their mates. I pray none of them are being mistreated.

"Tornn," I say, peering at the platter of meat. "Um, do you keep a large amount of livestock on your ship? I'm curious. I mean, on the *Jansonna*, we don't have *any* animals. Not as food or as pets. A few of the Founders brought cats, dogs, and other small creatures with them, but by the time I was born all the pets were gone. Feeding them was too difficult and the command team decreed that they wouldn't be permitted to breed. I've never seen an animal in real life. Only in photos and old movies."

He finishes the last of the meat he'd stabbed his fork into, chews and swallows quickly. His gaze remains riveted to me, and a flush spreads over my neck. Whenever he gives me his full attention, it never fails to make my heart pound faster as heated quivers assail my insides.

"We do not keep animals on our ships," he says. "In fact, we stopped keeping livestock long ago even on land. Instead, we use samples of cultivated animal cells to grow meat in a lab. It's more efficient." He leans forward, still holding my gaze. "The Founders? Are those the first humans who lived on the *Jansonna*?"

"Not exactly. Founders were wealthy humans who financed the construction of the *Jansonna*. My grand-parents were Founders. But the Founders only made up a small percentage of the humans who boarded the *Jansonna* on Death Day."

"Death Day?" He lifts an eyebrow, looking intrigued, and a thrill rushes through me that he's showing an interest in the history of my people.

"Oh, yes, Death Day," I say, feeling as though I'm slipping into teacher-mode. "A rather dramatic name, is it not?" I grin. "It's the deadline that the Frexorlians gave humans to evacuate Earth before they annihi-lated us. Actually, it was the Frexorlians who called it Death Day in the first place. On that day in history, the *Jansonna* remained on Earth until the last possible second in order to allow as many humans as possible to reach safety. Those who were left behind are presumed dead, killed by the filthy, planet-thieving Frexorlians."

Humor glints in Tornn's eyes and he looks like he's trying to restrain a smile, though I suppose I can't blame him. I always speak in an overly dramatic tone when I talk about Earth history, and I'm suddenly struck by how much I miss teaching.

"Five years before their arrival," I continue, "they started transmitting messages to Earth and gave us a specific date to evacuate by or face certain death. But there were a lot of political leaders and regular citizens who believed the Frexorlians weren't real. Many thought it must be a hoax of some sort, especially since the other aliens we'd already made contact with had never heard of them. The Founders were relentlessly teased for spending trillions of galactic credits on the construction of a worldship that might never be used."

"How many humans left Earth on the *Jansonna*?"

"Over one hundred thousand." I shudder to imagine how crowded the worldship was back then, but I take pride in knowing the Founders accepted almost anyone who could reach the vessel in time. They accepted criminals, the elderly, and the sick. Only those who were deemed too violent, highly contagious, or on the verge of death were barred from coming aboard.

Tornn draws back, his eyes flickering with surprise. "But the *Jansonna* currently houses over fifty-thousand humans. What happened? Why hasn't your population at least remained steady?"

"Unfortunately, not long after leaving Earth, a plague swept through the worldship, and thousands died. Then, during the early years, the command team eventually gained more power than the Founders, and they instituted strict rules regarding reproduction."

"Ah. The hormone suppression shots."

"Yes," I say, "but they also force couples to apply for a permit to have a baby, and nearly all children are conceived in a fertility lab. Only a certain number of permits are granted each year and the application process is rigorous." A dark heaviness falls over me as I think about Nathan. We'd already started filling out our application even though we hadn't gotten married yet. The future I thought I would share with him will never come to pass.

Yet if a future with Nathan was offered to me at this very second, I wouldn't take it. It's not what I want anymore, and I'm starting to realize he's not the man I once thought he was.

Traitor. Whore.

The insults he'd texted me flash in my mind. We haven't spoken since.

"Ellie? Sweet human?" Tornn's eyes gleam with concern. "Are you all right? You appear suddenly pale."

I force a smile. "Oh, I'm perfectly fine." I swallow hard, all at once desperate to change the subject. After drawing in a deep, calming breath, I say, "Tell me about your homeworld, Tornn."

He tenses as his expression transforms completely, all hints of warmth vanishing, cold rage now glimmering in his eyes. My fork slips from my fingers and clatters to the table. I don't think he's upset with me, but I realize I've inadvertently touched on a difficult subject.

His homeworld… is it gone?

My mouth goes dry, and I don't have the courage to ask. So, I sit very still and watch him carefully, wondering if he'll answer my question. My mind runs wild with terrible scenarios… his planet destroyed by an asteroid or stolen by a more powerful race of aliens. Another idea hits me.

Maybe whatever happened to the Darrvason females is linked to the loss of their homeworld.

I glance at the viewscreen, where I spot several ships as they travel alongside us in hyperspace, stars streaking by in blurs of bright light.

When Tornn finally speaks, his words shock me to my core.

"Darrvas, my people's homeworld, was destroyed by our enemies when I was a child. I was off planet visiting my father during the attack—at the time, he was the captain of the *Haxxal*." A faraway look enters his eyes, and his hands curl into fists.

I don't blink. I don't breathe as I wait for him to continue. Will he tell me more? I never imagined such a great tragedy had befallen the Darrvasons and my heart goes out to him. I'd wanted to ask about his homeworld since the day he selected me as his mate, but something had held me back, a vague feeling that perhaps I ought to avoid the subject.

"When our enemies—the Yelltzins—destroyed our

homeworld, there were no survivors. The fifteen ships in our fleet and those who were aboard are all that's left of our empire. Only a few females were off planet at the time, mostly wives and daughters of captains and officers. Not enough to prevent the demise of our race." His expression is pained, his eyes so haunted that I long to reach across the table and grasp his hand.

But he's become so tense during the last few seconds, his muscles bulging, his jaw clenched hard, that I worry touching him would be tantamount to kicking a bomb.

He draws in a deep breath and exhales slowly, and I'm relieved when his fists start unclenching. Some of the coldness leaves his eyes and he appears less forbidding than moments ago.

He meets my gaze. "We slaughtered them. The Yelltzins. We erased them from existence. We always, *always* hunt down our enemies."

Chapter 22

ELLIE

I'M RELIEVED WHEN TORNN LEAVES AFTER BREAKFAST. After he'd finished telling me about what happened to his homeworld and his people's females, I didn't quite know what to say.

'I'm so sorry' seems like a woefully inadequate response after someone tells you about the destruction of their homeworld. Yet that was all I said as Tornn sat across from me at the table, both of us still as statues, our meals forgotten.

Jenny would've known the right thing to say. She would've uttered something deep and touching.

God, how I miss her. I would give anything to speak with her again.

It seems unfair that I have a clear view of the *Jansonna* from the viewscreen in Tornn's quarters, yet I can't communicate with my family.

I swallow hard and rise from the table. I place the dirty dishes in the sanitation receptacle just before the android enters the kitchen, then aimlessly wander around my mate's living space.

Two weeks. I've belonged to Tornn for two weeks now, though it feels like so much longer. Sometimes I become so homesick that I find myself holding back tears. Other times I briefly forget about the life I left behind—that usually happens during my evenings spent with Tornn.

We slaughtered them. The Yelltzins. We erased them from existence. We always, always hunt down our enemies.

My mate's words from earlier keep replaying in my thoughts. There was already no doubt in my mind that the Darrvasons were powerful and could be deadly, but hearing Tornn admit they'd destroyed another race is jarring.

What would his people do to humankind if we crossed them the wrong way? I think of Nathan and whatever plot he's involved in and shiver. I still don't know if he had a hand in what happened with Officer Paddax.

Tornn remains infuriatingly secretive about Paddax and his mate, though I've since learned her name is Sheila. Whenever I bring up the topic, he insists it's being handled and that I have nothing to worry about because the alliance is still intact.

So much for my original plan to visit Sheila in the brig. I'm not sure if she's still incarcerated, nor do I have any idea whether Paddax remains in the medical bay.

With a frustrated sigh, I grab my reading tablet and settle on the plush sofa in front of the viewscreen. To my relief, there aren't any new messages from Nathan waiting on me.

In an effort to distract myself from present circumstances, I start perusing the reading material that's available to me.

The tablet contains thousands of history books, most of which I've already read, but as I swipe through the various covers, trying to decide what I'm in the mood for, I come across the hidden file that contains the banned romance novels I'd swiped from an old electronic library in the bowels of the *Jansonna*.

Do I dare read one?

I glance around Tornn's quarters, my heart racing.

Though I'm no longer aboard the worldship, I can't help but worry that a morality officer is about to barge into the room and arrest me for indecency. Nathan's cousin is a morality officer, and my skin crawled whenever I was in his presence as I worried he would somehow discover my illegal reading habits.

Logically, I know the only person who will enter Tornn's quarters is Tornn himself. Even the workers who deliver his fresh meat every evening don't come inside. They ring the bell, hand over the goods, and I barely catch a glimpse of them.

After a steadying breath, I select a historical romance novel that was always one of my favorites. It contains numerous detailed passages of sexual activities, including a rather scandalous romp in a moving, horse-drawn carriage. Though the book has never caused me to experience arousal, I can't help but wonder if maybe now it will.

I'm off the hormone suppression shots, and I feel as though I'm in the midst of a carnal awakening. I've enjoyed myself every single time Tornn has claimed me. My face heats and warmth quakes in my core as I think about how he buries his face between my thighs and laps at my clit at least once a day.

Feeling naughty but also brave, I swipe open the illicit book and start reading. If I'm remembering correctly, the wedding night happens in the second chapter. With a sigh of contentment, I snuggle deeper into the sofa and read faster.

———

TORNN

"IF YOU WILL ALL TAKE A LOOK AT THE DATA," I SAY IN the calmest tone I can muster, "I'm confident you'll find Planet 58-Zallnanis is a perfect candidate not only for humankind's occupation, but for the Darrvason Empire as well. Given that there are six large continents, that leaves us with plenty of space to spread out. We can reside on a continent far from wherever the humans create their first settlement."

Advisor Bemment snorts. "And live in close proximity to a race that's tried to infect us with a deadly virus? No thank you."

Some of the advisors at the table murmur their

agreement, while others shake their heads and voice their opposition to Advisor Bemment's views. Emperor Radakk, who sits at the head of the long table, appears deep in thought, though I cannot discern whether he supports my viewpoint.

"While I can understand your concern, Advisor Bemment," I say, "I am confident that the humans won't pose a threat to us. Our weaponry and our technology are far superior to theirs, as is our medical knowledge. By my estimations, we are at least three thousand years ahead of them in all major developments."

"And what happens in three thousand years, then?" the disagreeable advisor blurts. "I don't want the humans showing up on my great-grandchildren's doorstep and blasting them to pieces! I won't have it! I say we see the humans settled on 58-Z, then once we acquire the remaining females they have promised us, we will set off to search for a planet more to our liking. A long-term plan is a better one, Admiral Tornn."

Advisor Yumuf, an old friend of my father's, scoffs and gives Bemment a dirty look. "Perhaps in three thousand years the humans will be just as advanced as we are now, but where do you think *we'll* be in three thousand years? Do you honestly think we'll be frozen in time? Do you think we'll fail to continue making scientific advancements? There are times, Advisor Bemment, that I'm afraid the rumors about you are true—that you have rodent excrement for brains."

I bite back a grin as an argument erupts, about two thirds of the advisors backing Yumuf and the rest backing Bemment. My spirits lift when I realize my viewpoint holds the majority. Of course, Emperor Radakk has the final say.

"Why not raid the *Jansonna* for females, then take 58-Z for ourselves?" shouts Advisor Vobalt, a male I find even more repugnant than Bemment. But I'm shocked when it's Bemment who offers a rebuttal.

"Idiot!" Advisor Bemment roars as he stares Vobalt down from across the table. "Have you missed the entire point of us forging an alliance with the humans and offering payment for their females rather than stealing them? We are trying to start over, build a new life for ourselves that includes alliances and trade with other races. No one will trade with us if they believe we're duplicitous."

"We will not repeat the mistakes of the past," Emperor Radakk says with a dark look at Vobalt, and the room goes deathly quiet. "Stealing the worldship's fertile females and then abandoning the rest of the humans to their ailing vessel is equal to blasting them to dust."

"You make a wise point, Emperor," Bemment says with a smug glance at Vobalt.

"Advisors, Emperor," I say with a nod of respect, wanting to redirect the conversation to the settlement of Planet 58-Z, "I beseech you to think about the human women we're taking as mates. I know from my own experience, and from speaking with other males who recently claimed a human female, that the women are reluctant to leave their family and friends behind. The women we're being given aren't volunteers. They are selected by *Jansonna's* command team, and they aren't given a choice."

"Who cares!" Advisor Bemment shouts. "They are females, and they will do as they're told."

I shoot him a severe look that causes him to sink lower in his chair, then I continue with the speech I'd prepared, hoping the emperor will think of his own female's happiness. "If we occupy the same planet as humankind, our new brides will be able to maintain contact and perhaps visit their family members. Such an arrangement would be beneficial to us because it's in our best interest to keep our females content. Content females will be better mothers."

Emperor Radakk sits taller in his chair. "My mate has requested to speak with her friends who are still aboard the *Jansonna*, and I promised her I would arrange it. I'd intended to ask you, Admiral Tornn, to arrange for video comms to be installed on the *Jansonna*. The engineers who are still making repairs on the human worldship should be able to do it. Anyway, my point is, I know how joyous it would make my mate if she could visit her friends from time to time. One day—very soon, I hope—she will birth my sons and daughters, and I feel an obligation to ensure her happiness."

Yes. A thrill rushes through me. The meeting is going in my favor. At any moment, I'm certain the emperor will announce his final decision. I exchange a quick look with Admiral Yumuf, who leans back in his chair with a haughty expression. Across the table, Admiral Bemment bristles, though he doesn't say another word. At least he knows when he's been beaten.

"I will arrange for video comms to be installed on the *Jansonna* immediately," I say. "I believe my mate would also enjoy the opportunity to speak with her family." Guilt hits me that the idea hadn't already occurred to me. I know Ellie misses her mother and sister. Her eyes fill with wistfulness whenever she speaks of them.

"Thank you, Admiral Tornn." Emperor Radakk rises to his feet, and the entire room stands up an instant later. The leader of the Darrvason Empire takes a deep breath and then says, "During the last twenty-five years, we've traveled through enough sectors and visited enough outposts to understand how rare it is to find an unspoiled planet. Most habitable planets are already occupied, and though we are certainly powerful enough to conquer a planet and take it for ourselves, I won't sanction the deaths of any more innocents."

There's a sudden heaviness to the room as we all remember what happened in the aftermath of the Yelltzins' attack on Darrvas. Most of us in the room were children at the time, but we witnessed our fathers and grandfathers destroy the Yelltzins' entire fleet as well as their homeworld, innocent citizens included. Millions of them. Though Emperor Radakk has never admitted it aloud, I suspect the order his father gave to eradicate the Yelltzins haunts him. It's one reason why the emperor would never sanction stealing humankind's females and then abandoning the remaining occupants of the *Jansonna* to certain death.

"Settling on 58-Z is our most logical choice," the emperor finally continues. "Not only to ensure the happiness of our mates, but for the future of our empire itself. If we need more females, they'll be within easy reach." He turns to me. "How do you think Captain Warren and his command team will react to the news that we plan to share a planet with them?"

"I'm not certain, however, he won't have any say in the matter. I suggest we call a meeting with *Jansonna's* command team soon and inform them of the news." I smirk inwardly knowing I'm the last individual Captain Warren wants to see. Not long ago, I'd paid him a special visit and threatened to skin him alive if he harmed any of our newly acquired females' family members. I'd also appointed my trusted cousin, Officer Brute, to remain on the *Jansonna* as an observer to ensure the worldship captain behaved himself.

"Agreed." Emperor Radakk peers at an image of 58-Z that's displayed on a large screen on the wall. "I will make a fleet-wide announcement later today and inform our people of our plans. After twenty-five years of journeying through space, searching for females we are sexually compatible with while also looking for a new planet to call home, I suspect the news will be joyfully received."

Chapter 23

ELLIE

By the time I reach chapter ten, home of the infamous carriage scene, I'm sweltering and aching and can't seem to focus on the book any longer. I turn the tablet off and set it aside, then glance at the door. Will Tornn return soon?

As I shift in place, the heat pulsing in my core deepens. But even though my mate gave me permission to pleasure myself in his absence, I still hesitate to take action. The very idea fills me with shame. If I stroke my clit, Tornn will expect to hear about it. And if I don't tell him about it and he somehow finds out, he'll consider that an act of disobedience.

A quiver races across my bottom cheeks. The prospect of receiving a real punishment from him fills me with a strange mix of trepidation and longing.

But maybe... maybe I can keep it a secret. Maybe

if I bring myself to a quick climax and then immediately wash my hands—or better yet, take a long bath and use extra soap—he'll never know. I try but fail to brush aside the guilt that flows when I consider disobeying my mate.

I glance at the timepiece on the living room wall, a recent addition from Tornn to help me keep track of the Darrvason day, which mercifully lasts about the same as a twenty-four-hour human one. It's still rather early and even if he returns for the midday meal, I should have at least another hour to myself. Plenty of time for a quick rub followed by a thorough bath during which I can erase all evidence of my naughtiness.

Leaning back on the sofa, I close my eyes and spread my legs. I reach down the pants and panties I'm wearing and drag two fingers along my slit. *Mm. Feels good.* A moan escapes me as I dip into my core and spread the moisture overtop my throbbing clit.

I stroke and I stroke, but when a release starts approaching, I slow my caresses until the moment passes. For a reason I can't fathom, I suddenly want to draw out this experience, to take my time as I picture a sensual scenario in my mind and pleasure myself.

At first, I think about the wedding night scene from the book, but my thoughts quickly turn to my own first night spent with Tornn. Our first mating. How he'd stripped off my clothing, then turned me over his knee to frisk me, pumping his fingers into my pussy and my ass to make sure I wasn't hiding any contraband.

The spanking. I replay the spanking over and over in my mind as I continue pressing on my swollen clit, circling it and sometimes giving it light pinches.

Yes. Close. I'm so close.

I picture how Tornn held me over his lap with my bottom lifted high in the air, my thighs spread indecently as he alternated swatting my cheeks and rubbing them.

I writhe against my hand as I think about the moment my mate grasped my hips and surged into my center from behind, driving into me while his vibrating balls impacted my clit.

"Oh! Oh!" I cry out as a delicious wave of bliss steals over me and I ride it to completion. Once the last pulse fades, my legs feel weak and I'm too drained of energy to move or even open my eyes. I float in a state of deep relaxation, ignoring the little voice in the back of my mind that whispers I should hurry up and bathe.

But the sound of a throat being cleared breaks through my reverie. I gasp and open my eyes, immediately yanking my hand from my pants. I blink up at the large Darrvason male who's looming over me.

Tornn. Oh God. It's Tornn.

How much did he see? My heart races. Did he witness the entire shameful deed?

"Hello, Ellie." He steps closer and I lower my head, unable to look him in the eyes.

"Uh, hello, Tornn. I didn't hear you come in. You, um, caught me by surprise." My face flames and I'm not sure what to do with my tainted hand. A glance at my fingers shows they're glistening with my arousal. How absolutely mortifying. And the guilt... the guilt I experienced earlier over my decision to keep a secret from Tornn comes back full force. What have I done? Or rather, what was I planning to do?

Tornn takes a seat next to me, his huge muscular thigh brushing against my much smaller one. I start trembling as he grasps my chin and forces my gaze to his.

"You needn't look so guilty or feel so ashamed over touching yourself, sweet human." A glint of amusement enters his eyes, though he's quick to blink it away. I'm sure he finds my shame a strange thing indeed. But he didn't grow up on the *Jansonna* where kissing was considered improper and simply talking about sex could earn you a visit from a morality officer.

"I-I know I don't need to be ashamed of what I just did, Tornn, but I can't help it, and then getting caught by you right after I finished... um, how much did you see?" I hold my breath and pray he walked in at the very end.

"I believe I witnessed the whole thing," he says, stroking my hair. "I walked in just as you were laying back on the sofa. At first, I thought you meant to take a nap, but then I came closer and heard you whimpering and moaning, and the delicious scent of your arousal reached me soon after." He takes a deep breath through his nose and releases a low, satisfied growl.

"I'm sorry," I blurt. "I didn't mean for you to see it."

He grasps my hand and brings my glistening fingertips to his lips. His tongue darts out and he slowly licks my digits clean. His eyes roll back in his head, and he gives another growl.

Heated tingles quake through me and godfucking-dammit but I'm becoming aroused all over again. I press my thighs tightly together as I fight the urge to squirm in place.

"You don't need to apologize, sweet human. You're allowed to pleasure yourself as long as you always tell me about it afterward, remember?"

My stomach lurches. "Yes," I force out. "I remember."

He places a finger beneath my chin and stares into my eyes for so long, I can't seem to stop shaking. I feel like he's reading my mind and discovering all my secrets. A tiny whimper escapes my throat, and I'm certain my guilt must be written all over my face.

"I'm going to ask you a question, Ellie, and I want you to be completely honest with me," he says, and my trepidation grows. "Did you plan to tell me that you touched yourself, or did you plan to keep it a secret?"

Tears burn in my eyes and my lips quiver. "I planned to keep it a secret. I'm so sorry." My voice breaks over the last few words.

I don't understand why, but I can't lie to him. Not when he's holding my gaze while asking a direct question. It feels too wrong. God help me if he ever catches me texting on my tablet.

He wipes at my cheeks, and I realize a few tears have fallen. I just admitted to planning to deceive him, yet he's tenderly wiping my tears away. I blink rapidly and swallow hard, praying for strength.

Surely he intends to chastise me.

He's going to cause me pain, and maybe… maybe I need it.

The air crackles with tension as I wait and wait for him to announce my fate.

At last, he drops his hand from my chin and rises to his feet. He peers down at me with a severe look that causes my insides to tremble. More than ever, I'm aware of his massive size and his brute strength.

"I appreciate that you just made a full confession. However, I cannot ignore that you planned to deceive me," he finally says, and there's a dangerous edge to his voice, a steely glint to his eyes, "and I will not tolerate an errant mate." He crosses his arms over his broad, muscular chest. "Go to the bedroom and remove all your clothing. I will join you in a moment to administer your punishment."

Chapter 24

TORNN

WHEN I ARRIVE IN THE BEDROOM, I FIND A gloriously naked Ellie waiting beside the bed.

My shafts thicken at the sight of her. We've been mated for fourteen days now, but every time I glimpse her unclothed body is like the first time.

She shoots me a pensive look as she twists her fingers together and steps from foot to foot. So nervous, my pretty little mate.

Her eyes bulge when she notices a strap dangling from my hand. She takes a step back, and as she shakes her head, her dark locks shift over her shoulders.

"Please, Tornn," she whispers, her gaze on the strap. "I-I don't think I misbehaved badly enough to warrant a whipping."

I flex the implement in my hands, feeling the

supple leather and admiring the craftsmanship. After I'd sent Ellie to the bedroom to await her punishment, I'd retrieved the strap which I'd had hidden away in a secret cabinet.

As I approach my bride, she takes several more steps away, but I soon have her cornered between the bed and the wall. I grasp her chin, forcing her to look into my eyes, wanting her to see my disappointment.

After setting the strap on the bed, I reach between her thighs and cup her slick pussy. "You planned to deceive me, Ellie. I think that deserves a whipping. Perhaps not a severe one, but you will feel the sting of my strap."

She whimpers but doesn't argue or plead with me to change my mind. Her capitulation pleases me, and a sense of responsibility falls over me as I hold her mesmerizing blue gaze. As her mate, it's my duty to guide her in the proper behavior of a wife. Wives aren't supposed to lie or keep secrets from their husbands.

"I plan to take you over my lap and spank you, sweet human, and once your bottom is bright red and well-punished, I will finish up with the strap. Cooperate during your spanking and I'll only give you five lashes with the strap." I stroke a digit through her wetness, and she shudders.

"Please," she begs again, but before she can say more, I lightly pinch her clit. She whimpers and thrusts her center into my hand, her hips undulating as I tease her button with gentle strokes.

I lean down and place my lips at her ear. "I like it

when you beg, sweet human. Your pleading always makes my cocks so *fluxxing* hard."

Her breath hitches and she rises on her tiptoes as I pinch her clit again. The scent of her excitement is heavy in the air. She's nervous, perhaps even a bit frightened, but she's also aching and trembling with need.

I release her chin and step back to push my sleeves up. She swallows hard and fidgets in place as she casts an uneasy glance at the strap. I sink down on the bed and draw her closer, forcing her to stand between my spread legs as I focus on her slick center. Her arousal gleams on her pussy lips and her inner thighs.

I nudge at the seam of her folds. "Did you really think I wouldn't find out, Ellie? Did you really think I wouldn't be able to smell your lingering wetness when I returned to my quarters?"

Her look of guilt increases, but she doesn't reply.

I give her a dark glare, retract my hand from her pussy, then swat her nether lips with the flat of my fingers. She gasps and tries to step back, but I grab her by the hips, forcing her to remain in place.

"I asked you a question, little female, and I expect an answer." I release one of her hips just long enough to deliver another swat to her pussy lips.

A pained look crosses her face, and I sense she doesn't want to answer. I lift my hand, preparing to strike her again, when she blurts out, "I-I planned to take a long bath after I finished touching myself."

Instead of swatting her pussy, I give it several light

pats as she quivers in place, needy whimpers occasionally escaping her throat.

I wait until she meets my gaze, then I say, "That was very naughty of you, Ellie. It would seem you put a lot of thought into your plan to keep a secret from me."

"I'm sorry," she whispers as I continue tapping at her folds. Her center lurches toward my touch several times, and I finally pause to carefully splay her petals apart so I might better glimpse her engorged clit.

"I believe that you're sorry," I say, "but I still intend to punish you, sweet human. I want to make sure you never consider deceiving me again, that you never consider keeping secrets from me."

I guide her over my lap and situate her upon one knee, then put my other leg atop hers, securing her in place. I nudge her thighs wider apart and cup her bottom, admiring her swollen pink parts. Some of the tension leaves her body as I continue massaging her backside. But she soon stiffens when I splay her cheeks apart with one hand, exposing her snug hole. I tap at the pucker as it winks several times.

"Look at this tight little hole. One day, I will pound you here," I say, pressing more firmly to the hole in question. "One day, I will shove inside both your holes at the same time."

She makes an alarmed noise in her throat as a tremor courses through her. "But I'm so tight back there, Tornn. How could you possibly…" Her voice trails off, and when I brush her hair aside to better glimpse her face, I find she's blushing profusely.

"Starting very soon, we will have nightly training sessions. I will replicate a set of plugs for your bottom, and we'll start with one of the smallest." I straighten, press a hand to the small of her back, and cup her ass. "I hope you'll remember to cooperate during your spanking. If you accept your punishment gracefully—without thrashing around and fighting me—you'll only receive five lashes of the strap. Show me what an obedient little female you can be." I bring my palm down on her left cheek with a resounding crack.

Chapter 25

ELLIE

I TRY TO REMAIN STILL AS TORNN PUNISHES ME WITH quick, hard smacks to my bottom. Shame courses through me when I think about my plans to disobey him, and there's a part of me that's glad I was caught. Because now he's helping expunge my guilt, he's chastising me for the wrong I intended to commit. I try not to think about the other secrets I'm keeping from him.

Not for the first time, I wonder why I'm so eager to please him. Why I can't bear to lie to his face.

My ass is ablaze and he keeps on spanking. The pain brings tears to my eyes. I writhe slightly on his lap —I can't help it—and I immediately become aware of the huge, hard bulge beneath my center. His cocks. Just like the other two times he's spanked me, he's getting aroused as he punishes me.

But he's not the only one.

Heated pulses surge through my core even as the sting pelting my cheeks intensifies, even as I struggle to breathe through the searing blows. My clit starts throbbing and I'm certain my pussy must be soaked by now. Draped over his knee with my thighs parted wide, I know he has an unhindered view of my nether parts.

He pauses to caress my bottom, and I pray he's done. I pray it's almost over, even though I dread the whipping to come. Five lashes. He plans to give me five lashes. How badly will it hurt?

"I'm your mate, Ellie, your master," he says as he continues rubbing my ass. "You must never, ever keep secrets from me. You must never plan to deceive me. I won't tolerate lies or lies by omission. I won't tolerate disobedience. Do you understand, little female?"

"Yes," I reply, my voice cracking. "Yes, I understand." Again, I push thoughts of Nathan's texts out of my mind, telling myself it's a problem for another day.

It's on the tip of my tongue to beg Tornn not to follow through with the whipping, but I stop myself as a wave of surrender crashes over me. I know it's going to hurt, but I want to accept the remainder of my punishment.

I'm desperate to assuage the lingering remnants of guilt, and I also long to be back in Tornn's good graces. I crave his forgiveness beyond all reason, and I'm almost eager for the first searing lash of the strap across my bottom cheeks.

Tornn lifts me off his lap and stands behind me as he guides me into position over the bed. My ass is throbbing and I long to reach back and rub out the sting, but I don't dare. Not when he's watching. Not when he's about to wield the strap.

He grasps my wrists and pulls my arms out in front of me, then retrieves a soft black binding from his pocket and ties the fabric around my wrists. My heart beats faster and my stomach dips. He hasn't picked the strap up yet, and it's in my line of vision. I can't stop looking at it.

Waves of heat roll off Tornn's huge, muscular body as he leans over me, brushing my hair from my face, not allowing me to hide from him. He checks the binding on my wrists again as his breath dances over my earlobe.

"I want to make sure you don't reach back to shield your bottom, little female. I don't want your hands getting hurt." His voice is gentle, almost... caring. It brings tears to my eyes because this is the final part of my punishment, and absolution hovers just within reach.

As he goes for the strap, I casually test the bindings. They're secure but not uncomfortably tight. I can't escape them, but they're not cutting off my circulation. Warmth fills me as I realize the care he'd taken while binding my wrists, and I'm reminded that while he's a demanding male who expects my obedience, he hasn't yet treated me with cruelty. I pray he never does.

A shiver rushes down my back as he trails the strap

over my bottom cheeks. I whimper and tense, expecting the first lash to fall at any moment. But he continues trailing the implement over my flesh for some time, content to draw out my punishment. Or maybe he's giving me a chance to catch my breath after the spanking.

At some point as he trails the strap over my flesh, my anticipation starts to build anew. I'm nervous about the five lashes I have coming, but my yearning for absolution is so intense, I almost lift my bottom in invitation of the first strike.

The aching in my core becomes stronger as he continues teasing me with the strap. When he nudges my thighs wider apart and runs a digit through my wetness, I quiver and my center jolts backward. Ignoring my pulsing clit, he inserts two fingers into my pussy, driving in and out, building a delicious rhythm that has me releasing a needy moan. My face flames as I undulate my hips in tune with his ministrations.

"I should be whipping you right now, little female," he says in a deeper than usual voice, "but I cannot resist touching your swollen, pink parts. After your punishment is over, I expect you to reach back and pull your center apart for me. I expect you to spread your slick pussy wide for my claiming."

His crass words cause little quivers to assail me, and though I should be outraged by his intention to pound me after he punishes me, it feels like a part of my penance. And I welcome it. I want it. I'm fucking aching for it even as my nervousness over the pain of the whipping escalates with each passing second.

I swallow hard when he abruptly withdraws his fingers from my core and steps back. It's time. He's about to bring the strap down across my already stinging ass cheeks.

There's a sudden whoosh and a crack followed by a shocking lash of pain. I cry out and pull against the bindings. I even try to push myself up, but I can't manage the movement because my toes barely reach the floor. Before I can suck in my next breath, he brings the strap down again.

"Please have mercy," I find myself saying through my tears, which are all at once flowing down my face. "Please not so hard."

He runs a hand lightly over my bottom, as though admiring his handiwork. A deep rumbling growl issues from his throat. He steps closer and presses his erections against my buttocks, allowing me to feel his immense bulge through his pants. He's rock hard and I easily detect the rapid vibration of his balls.

"Your sweet begging won't stay my hand, little female, but it will make my cocks fully erect, and it will make me ravenous to pound you." He thrusts his center forward a few times, undulating his huge bulge against my sore bottom.

A mournful cry escapes my lips when he steps away a few seconds later, taking the wondrous vibrations with him.

Another whoosh and I clench my cheeks as the strap cracks across my tenderized flesh. Three. I've endured three lashes thus far. I sniffle and whimper as I await the final two.

"*Please please please,*" I murmur through my tears, even though I know further begging is futile. Even though I know he revels in my desperate pleas. I try not to think about the dark part of him that savors my agony as he chastises me, the part of him that likes hearing me beg for mercy he has no intention of granting.

"I will always give you what you need, sweet human," he says, once again trailing the strap over my flesh. "Right now, you need absolution. You need pain and you need tears, and you also need my cocks deep inside you, pounding you, filling you up and reminding you that you *fluxxing* belong to me. Lastly, you need to feel my seed trickling out of your sore, well-fucked pussy."

Before I can finish processing his words, he administers the final two blows, bringing the strap down on my stinging buttocks as I writhe on the bed in a pointless attempt to avoid the lashing. A scream catches in my throat and more tears roll down my face.

My bottom is on fire, but despite the sting, I'm filled with relief. Because it's over and I survived and I'll never, ever disobey (or make plans to disobey) my mate again. That's what I tell myself, anyway.

Fuck fuck fuck. The texting program on my tablet. I must delete it and pretend the strained conversations with Nathan never happened. I must cut all ties with my former fiancé and pray whatever plot he's involved in never comes to fruition.

I hear a thud on the bed and blink my eyes open to find Tornn has tossed the strap near the pillows. I shudder as he caresses a gentle hand over my flaming backside, and when his finger goes in a straight line across my left cheek, I whimper as I realize he's tracing a welt.

"Remember what comes next, little female." His hand leaves my ass, and he leans over me to quickly unfasten the fabric binding my wrists. Then he steps away, and I feel his gaze searing into me as he awaits my final surrender.

My hands tremble as I reach back to grasp my sore bottom cheeks, taking one in each hand and spreading my center wide.

"That's it. More. A bit wider. Show me the slick, pink hole that belongs to me." His growls of pleasure reverberate off the walls.

Chapter 26

TORNN

I'M PLEASED BY MY MATE'S BEAUTIFUL SURRENDER AS she draws her reddened ass cheeks wide apart, revealing her puckering hole and her wet, swollen pussy. My blood heats and a fierce snarl rips from my throat. I quickly shed my clothing and approach Ellie from behind, fisting my lower appendage as a blue drop of my seed glistens on the bulbous tip.

After I position my cock at her gaping entrance, I pry her hands off her cheeks and gather her wrists in one hand, pressing them at the small of her back. "Good little female."

Without warning, I slam into her slick, tight channel. She gasps and writhes underneath me as I set a rapid, punishing rhythm of claiming her. I hold her down as I plunge into her pussy, taking what's mine.

My vibrating balls repeatedly slam into her engorged button.

"You belong to me, sweet human," I growl through clenched teeth, "you belong to me, and I want everyone to know it. I want to pump all your orifices full of my seed. Your tight pussy, your snug asshole, and your sweet mouth. I want every male who comes near you to know whose seed you're drenched in. *Fluxx.* Maybe I'll put my seed in a vial and force you to wear it around your pretty little neck."

It doesn't take long for her inner walls to contract around my thick length, and I groan at the sensation as she cries out during the throes of her climax. I release her wrists and guide her hands in front of her, allowing her to rest, but only briefly. I intend to keep pumping into her with my lower appendage until I spurt my essence deep inside her, then I plan to pound her again with my upper shaft as my vibrating balls continue smacking into her clit.

Once her breathing starts to regulate, I commence driving into her with fast strokes, my gaze on the five distinct stripes across her thoroughly punished bottom cheeks. Her flesh is slightly welted, though I doubt the marks will last long. Perhaps two or three days.

My cocks harden further and my lower one erupts inside her as a quaking wave of bliss sweeps over me. After the last pulsing spurt of my essence fills her, I withdraw from her center and immediately shove my upper shaft into her seed-drenched hole.

She cries out as another orgasm seizes her, and I watch with satisfaction as she grips the covers so hard her knuckles turn white. Her hair flails around her shoulders as she tosses her head from side to side, shuddering as I pause in my thrusts but remain submerged deep within her, allowing my balls to vibrate directly upon her clit while she shatters.

I find my own release a moment later. Her insides gripping my upper shaft makes it impossible to maintain control, and I once again fill her with my essence, riding her to completion, until the final quaking spurt releases from my body.

Breathless from my exertions, I withdraw from her center and carefully lift her in my arms. The urge to hold her close and see to her comfort is overwhelming. I carry her to a nearby chair and sink down in the cushions, arranging her on my lap, cradling her limp form in my arms. As she sits on me, the seed I'd just spurted into her leaks onto my thighs, but I don't care. I need to have her close. I need to… tend to her.

I brush her hair from her face and study her expression. Her eyes are closed, but I can easily sense her exhaustion. I peer at the tear tracks on her cheeks and lean closer, darting out my tongue as I reverently lick the tears from her face. Her eyes shoot open, and she gives a tiny gasp as she draws back, clearly surprised by my actions.

As she holds my gaze, the ancestral markings across my chest start tingling. It's not the first time it's happened in her presence, and I doubt it will be the last. But maybe it's a sign. A sign that we're becoming as bonded as we can be even though she's human and I'm Darrvason.

I can't deny that I crave her every moment of every day. I also can't deny that I'm eager to return to my quarters whenever time permits, even if it's only to enjoy a quick meal with her before I must return to my duties as admiral. Her presence both calms and invigorates me, and I'm starting to understand why our elders destroyed the Yelltzins' homeworld in a brutal act of revenge.

If something ever happened to Ellie... if someone stole her from me, I would tear up the universe looking for her. And I would maim and kill anyone who dared to cause her harm or worse. My chest tightens as I imagine her perishing at the hands of some unknown enemy.

A shaky breath leaves her, and she swallows hard. We're still staring at one another, and I'm *fluxxing* lost in her blue depths. Lost in her sweetness. I cup the side of her face, and to my great pleasure, she leans into my touch. Her eyes flutter shut, and she releases a soft sigh.

You are becoming precious to me, little female.

The words linger on my tongue, but I can't quite voice my thoughts aloud. I never expected to harbor such intense devotion and possessiveness for my human female. But with each passing day, my fixation with her becomes stronger, bordering on obsession.

"Are you all right, sweet human?" I ask instead.

She opens her eyes and a smile tugs at her lips. "My bottom hurts. And my pussy is a bit sore. But I'm okay." She pauses and a look of uncertainty falls over

her. "I'm truly sorry I planned to disobey you. Am I…
forgiven?"

"Yes, Ellie. All is forgiven." I'd forgiven her before
I'd taken her over my knee, yet I'd still chastised her.
Because she'd needed it, and because I'd wanted to
ensure she never repeated the offense. Still cupping
her face, I stroke her chin with my thumb. "Do you
feel absolved of your sins, little female, or do you
require more punishment, more pain?"

She inhales a quivering breath. "I feel absolved,"
she says as a fresh blush tinges her cheeks.

I nod and gather her deeper in my arms, holding
her tight as my ancestral markings tingle harder than
ever before.

Chapter 27

ELLIE

I CAN'T STOP SCRATCHING MY ARMS. PEERING IN THE bathroom mirror, I gaze at my inflamed flesh as I debate whether to mention the issue to Tornn. No doubt he would insist I see a doctor, but the idea of being examined by a Darrvason physician makes me nervous, though I'm not sure why. On the *Jansonna*, I never had any qualms about going to the medical bay when necessary.

With a sigh, I glance down at my arms. Maybe I'm having an allergic reaction to something in Tornn's quarters. Hm. Perhaps it's the bedsheets. Or the material in the long-sleeved gowns he recently gifted me.

I pull the sleeves of the dress I'm wearing down to my wrists. It's late in the evening and Tornn will be returning at any moment. We'd already enjoyed dinner together, but he'd had some work to finish before he could retire for the night.

My heart races when I contemplate what will happen when he comes back. Yesterday, he'd mentioned training my bottom hole with plugs, stating that he would start training me *very soon*. Tonight, perhaps?

Anticipation builds from deep within, causing my breath to quicken and warm quaking pulses to afflict my center. I exit the bathroom and walk around his quarters, wondering when he'll let me roam the ship whenever I want. Without his escort. I'm eager to explore the *Haxxal* and anxious to speak with Sheila. I'm not certain if she's still in the brig—Tornn is reluctant to answer my questions, and whenever I inquire about the situation, he simply insists it's being handled and promises the alliance is still intact.

Will he ever trust me enough to talk about his work with me? It's a bit jarring that he's allowed to keep secrets, but apparently, I'm not. If he asks me a question, he expects an honest answer immediately.

Of course, there's that big secret I'm still keeping from him. *Nathan. Nathan and his vague fucking asinine messages.* I've never breathed a word about my former fiancé to Tornn.

If I'm being honest, I'm scared of his reaction if he finds out I used to be in love with another man.

Wait a second—*used to be in love? Used to?*

After I search my heart, I realize it's true. I no longer hold Nathan in high regard, and it's not just because he'd recently called me names. In truth, I think we'd started growing apart even before I was told I would become a Darrvason bride.

But no matter my current feelings for Nathan, as possessive as Tornn is, I'm afraid he might find a way to hurt my former fiancé, even if such an action goes against the terms of the alliance.

I resolve that I'll keep this one secret no matter what. I promise myself I'll lie to his face if he ever asks about my past romantic history. I doubt it'll matter to him that I never slept with Nathan, that our relationship never went beyond cuddling on the sofa together. Oh, and the one and only kiss we shared, anticlimactic as it was.

Exhaustion weighs me down and my eyelids start to feel heavy. With great care, I ease onto the bed but don't get under the covers, promising myself I'm just taking a quick rest and I'm not calling it a night yet. I make sure to curl up on my side. My bottom is too tender from yesterday's punishment to sit comfortably or lay on my back.

I reach around and gingerly feel my ass, moving from cheek to cheek as I test the soreness.

"Here, sweet human, let me help you," comes a deep, masculine voice from the doorway, catching me by surprise.

I suppress a gasp and start to rise from the bed, only for Tornn to hurry forward and place a hand on my shoulder, forcing me to remain in place.

"I'm sorry if I scared you." His eyes are warm, and he's holding a clear jar that's filled with an orange substance. "I'm late getting back, and I thought you might be asleep, so I was careful to keep my footsteps quiet."

I focus on the jar. "What's that?"

"A numbing salve." He guides me onto my stomach, then slowly draws up my gown and pulls my panties down, baring my bottom. "Let me rub it into your sore cheeks, sweet human."

"Okay," I whisper, touched by the gesture. Also shocked.

He gives me a tender look and caresses a hand through my hair, and I'm not sure what to think. But I like this side of him. I've seen glimpses of his gentle side before, but this is by far his most compassionate gesture. I'd gotten the marks on my bottom because I'd planned to disobey him, but now that I've paid my penance, he seems eager to alleviate my discomfort.

I watch as he opens the jar and scoops out a generous amount of the orange salve. A minty scent fills the air. After setting the jar aside, he creates a lather with his hands and the substance becomes thicker but also translucent.

He settles beside me on the mattress and starts applying the salve to my cheeks with the softest of caresses. My throat suddenly burns and I'm not sure why. And my arms are itching again. It's taking all my self-control not to thrash around and start scratching them.

Hm. Maybe later I can rub some of the numbing salve onto my arms.

Tucking this thought away, I try to enjoy the sensation of Tornn massaging my ass. The soreness fades until there's no pain left.

"Feeling better yet?" His eyes flicker with more warmth, and dammit his sweetness might make me cry. He's taking care of me the way Nathan used to if I was sick or overly fatigued after a long day of teaching. He's being *kind*.

"Yes," I whisper, "the pain is gone. Thank you, Tornn."

He doesn't smile, but the warmth that lights his eyes takes my breath away. He gives a light tug on the sleeve of my dress. "Let's get this off you so you can go to bed."

My throat burns as he guides me into a sitting position just long enough to pull the gown, which is bunched up around my waist, over my head. It's not until his eyes widen that I realize my blunder. I should've turned the lights down so he wouldn't notice the scratch marks on my arms.

His nostrils flare and his jaw tenses, though he appears more shocked, perhaps even a tad confused, than angry. He grasps my upper arms and pulls me closer as he inspects the markings, running a gentle hand over the redness that mars my skin. His eyes widen and he sits back, absently rubbing a hand over his upper chest.

"What happened?" he asks with a nod at my arms.

I shrug and give a brief shake of my head. "I'm not sure. My arms have been itchy for the last few days. I'm probably allergic to something." My mouth goes dry when his eyes flash as though he's about to scold me or accuse me of something, but I can't imagine what I might've done wrong.

"You should've told me, Ellie." He lifts his wrist comm to his mouth and speaks in Darrvason, issuing what sounds like a terse command. A vein in his temple pulses as he stares at me, and his entire body stiffens.

"I'm sorry. I didn't think it was a big deal." I brush a hand along my arm, trying to resist the urge to scratch, and I glance at the jar of numbing salve.

"Your health is important to me," he says in a matter-of-fact tone, "as you are the female who will bear my sons and daughters. I've summoned a physician and he'll be here soon."

The burning in my throat intensifies and I pretend to be very interested in smoothing out the wrinkles in the bedcovers. He doesn't care about the rashes on my arms because he cares for me. He only cares for the children I will bear.

Breeding purposes.

That's all he wants me for. I knew why the Darrvasons wanted human women, but hearing Tornn confirm it aloud breaks my heart, and all the warmth I'd experienced as he gently rubbed numbing salve into my backside vanishes. Surely I imagined the affectionate look he'd given me as he tended to my sore bottom.

Tornn rises from the bed and grasps my discarded gown. Then he abruptly tears the sleeves from it and tosses it at me. "Put this on immediately. I don't want the doctor looking upon you entirely unclothed unless it's absolutely necessary." He runs a hand through his hair and paces the bedroom as I slip back into the gown.

Suddenly, I'm heartsick for the *Jansonna*. I miss my mother and sister and friends and students so much it hurts to breathe. And I'm angry that I don't miss Nathan. I'm angry that the gentle love we once shared has been fucking ruined by the Darrvasons and the goddamn alliance.

As my despair deepens, I realize what I want more than anything—to mean something to someone. But I'll never have that with Tornn. I'm nothing but an incubator to him. A possession.

Chapter 28

TORNN

I FINISH DRAWING THE COVERS OVER ELLIE, WHOSE arms are no longer inflamed thanks to a medication the physician administered by hypospray. She's still wearing the gown with the ripped sleeves, but I don't want to remove her clothing for bed while there's another male in my quarters, even if the male in question is both a physician and an old friend of mine.

"Is everything all right?" Her eyes flash with worry as she glances toward the door. "Please tell me what the doctor said. Am I sick or is it an allergic reaction like I thought?" She swallows hard and blinks rapidly.

Guilt settles over me. I'd purposely conversed with the physician in Darrvason as he examined her, not wanting her to understand the questions I'd asked. Questions that haven't yet been answered. The physician is currently in the main sitting area of my quarters as he examines the results of the various tests he'd run with his scanner.

"The doctor is not certain what caused the itching; however, I am confident that he will discover what ails you very soon. He's reading the results of your tests as we speak." I stroke a hand through her hair, hesitant to leave her side even though I'm anxious to discover if the physician has made any breakthroughs yet. "The medication he administered should last for about five days and keep your arms from itching. If the discomfort continues once the medication wears off, the doctor will return to give you another shot."

"What if it's a weird alien virus," she says. "When was the last time your ship docked at an outpost? When was the last time any of your people interacted with another species? It's possible one of your people, perhaps even you, is silently carrying an alien virus that you picked up at an outpost and inadvertently transmitted it to me." She bolts upright and pushes the covers down, a sense of panic surrounding her. "Are other human women experiencing similar symptoms?"

"I doubt it's an alien virus," I say, placing a hand on her shoulder, hoping to calm her. "It's been several moon cycles since any of my people have interacted with another species at an outpost, but we have strict decontamination procedures in place. Please do not worry. I'm certain the doctor will soon learn what's ailing you and devise a suitable treatment."

"That's how my father died." Her face goes pale and her lips tremble. I have the sudden urge to take her in my arms, but I hesitate when I hear the physician clearing his throat as though to summon me. He must've found something.

"Your father perished from an alien virus he acquired on an outpost?" I ask gently.

She nods and blinks fast. "He served as an emissary whenever we made contact with new alien races. He spent a week on the Gervaxxan Outpost as he tried to forge an alliance with anyone who might be able to provide us with fuel. He succeeded in his mission, but not long after his return to the *Jansonna*, despite all the precautions he took, he still fell ill. So did the advisors who accompanied him. Every last one of them died."

A tear rolls down her cheek. I try to wipe it away, but she draws back from me and does it herself. A tremor racks her tiny body as she lowers her head, avoiding my gaze.

"I am sorry for what happened to your father, sweet human. But I promise the same will not happen to you."

"You never answered my question about the other human brides. Am I the only one experiencing these symptoms, or are there others?" She wraps her arms around her center, her shaking increasing, and as I hear the physician clear his throat a second time, I'm torn between staying to comfort my mate or leaving her side to obtain answers from the male. As the admiral of the Darrvason fleet, it's my obligation to quickly ascertain if there's a health risk to my people and the other human females. But for the first time in my life, my sense of duty wars with my heart.

"I don't know if you're the only one experiencing symptoms, Ellie, but I will ask the doctor in a moment." I try to guide her underneath the covers so I might tuck her in again, but she resists my efforts and moves to the other side of the bed, shooting me an enraged look.

"I know I'm *just a female* to you, someone to fuck and impregnate as many times as you can, but I'm also a fucking person, *Admiral* Tornn," she says, using a mocking voice as she utters my title. Intentionally showing me disrespect.

I'm so stunned by her words that for a long moment, all I can do is stare at her. Her tone and crass language are unacceptable for a female to use while speaking to her mate. Surely she must know that. I take a long breath as I try to settle the rage that simmers under my skin. I don't understand her rebelliousness or her anger, but I will not suffer an unruly female.

"Come here." I crook a finger at her, then pat the space she'd just vacated.

Her hair flips wildly about her shoulders as she shakes her head. "Why? So you can put me to bed and then go speak to the doctor about whatever's wrong with me out of my earshot, never mind that I can't understand the Darrvason tongue?" She scoffs. "It's my health yet it seems you want to keep me in the dark. Why must you be so secretive about everything? I've lost count of the times you've refused to answer my questions or changed the subject when I ask you something, especially when I inquire about Paddax and Sheila. You said I wasn't your prisoner, yet that's how I feel. I've been locked in your quarters for over two weeks now, only to be let out for brief walks through nearly empty corridors." Tears coat her face and she shudders. "I want to go home. I want to return to the *Jansonna*."

May the Star Gods strike the physician down because the rotten *ufullma* clears his throat for the third *fluxxing* time in a row. I stare at Ellie as I process her words, still shocked by her outburst.

But the most shocking thing of all is her proclamation that she wants to return to the human worldship. I seethe with fury over the prospect of letting her go.

I launch myself at her, easily forcing her onto the mattress beneath me as I cage her in, forcing her to hold my gaze. She fights me, swatting at my chest and thrashing in my arms. I secure her wrists in one hand and pin them above her head, then grip her chin and release a thunderous growl that causes her to go utterly still.

"You are mine!" I roar, breathing hard, filled with rage that she would dare ask to leave me. "We are mated, and Darrvasons mate for life."

"I'm not Darrvason," she whispers.

I release her wrists and grasp her upper arms, intending to shake her, but pause when a faint red symbol glimmers to life on her flesh. She follows my gaze and gasps, then immediately looks at my chest where my ancestral symbols are located beneath my shirt.

Feral need rips through me, and my cocks go hard,

my balls vibrating at a rapid speed. I'm straddling her, but I rearrange us on the bed so I'm positioned at her spread thighs. A snarl leaves me as I thrust against her. She whimpers and her hips jerk forward. Her arousal floods the air, a bouquet of feminine sweetness I could lose myself in.

Another symbol appears on her arm, close to the first one. I rip my shirt off and toss it aside. Her eyes widen when she looks from the new markings on her arm to those covering my chest. They are a perfect match to the first two symbols I wear. The ancestral symbols I was born with.

I'm vaguely aware of the physician leaving as footsteps sound in the entryway, followed by the door to my quarters zipping open and shut. With a shuddering sigh, I unfasten the front of my pants, releasing my shafts.

Ellie groans and digs her nails into my back as I drag my lower appendage through her increasing moisture. She gives her head a brief shake, as though to clear her thoughts, then traces the glowing red symbols on my chest. Pleasure quakes through me and I can't restrain another fierce growl.

"I'm furious with you, Tornn," she says, meeting my eyes as she continues trailing her fingers over my ancestral markings. "And I'm terrified. What's happening? Why do I want to take you inside me? Why am I suddenly tingling with warmth and longing?"

A third marking appears on her arm, and I trace it with my thumb, a deep satisfaction filling me. I never thought it possible, and the belief that we couldn't share a heartbond kept me from giving all of myself to her. It was why I frequently refused to answer her questions when she inquired about my past and why I hesitated to tell her about the happenings on the ship.

She's my mate and she's supposed to live among my people for the rest of her life, yet I've been treating her like an outsider. I've been holding her at a distance, perhaps a bit cruelly, and now I feel like the biggest fool. She follows my gaze, and a shaky breath escapes her.

"Tornn?"

"The symbols that are appearing on your arm are a match to the ancestral markings that cover my chest. Soon, both your arms will be covered with them. It means you're *mine*, you unruly little female. It means a traditional Darrvason heartbond is forming between us." I lean down and nip at her chin with my sharp teeth. She moans and gyrates her slick center against the bulbous head of my largest shaft. "Now, spread those thighs a bit wider and show me how furious you are."

Chapter 29

ELLIE

By the time Tornn finishes pounding me with both his appendages and my pussy is sore and dripping with his seed, my left arm is completely covered in the glowing red symbols. A match to those on his chest. His ancestral markings. I can scarcely believe it.

A heartbond. My stomach bottoms out. *Heartbond* sounds permanent. It sounds like forever. All my hopes of returning to the *Jansonna* fade, yet I'm not as upset over the prospect of never returning to my people as I was a few minutes ago.

I don't think it's love. It can't be love. But it's fucking powerful. A warmth and a longing that I can't deny. As though my soul is tethered to his for all time. The waves of submission I often experience in his presence are coming stronger. His physical strength and his dominance send a thrill through me. I like that he's holding me tight on his lap, stroking my hair as he keeps smelling my neck and dragging his tongue along my earlobes. Whenever I squirm, he tightens his hold and growls.

"I have never known such a calmness in my soul," he murmurs into my ear, his breath warm and sweet. "I never knew a heartbond would feel like this. My people believe it's not possible to share a heartbond with a non-Darrvason, but we are proof that it's possible." He growls. "When this becomes common knowledge among my people, all our males will want a human female of their own."

Despite the warmth that pervades my senses, a little alarm bell rings in my head. "How many unmated males are in your fleet?"

"Over twenty thousand."

"There aren't that many women of childbearing age on the *Jansonna*. Even if you claimed every last one of them, not all Darrvason males would get a mate." I pause and draw in a long breath. "What's happened between us—the heartbond—once this becomes common knowledge among your people, will it put the alliance in danger? Will your males want to raid the *Jansonna* for fertile females?" Coldness rushes over me as I think about Jenny.

"I must confess, sweet human, that I'm having difficulty thinking clearly right now. But you make a good point and it's a topic I'll put more thought into later. I promise I'll do everything in my power to maintain the alliance, however, any renegotiations will involve significant compensation to humankind."

"But you want more women," I say. "You want to tear more families apart. You want to *buy* us and treat us like property."

His nostrils flare and he tenses. "You belong to me, Ellie, yes, I won't deny that you're my possession. But I will protect you and do everything in my power to ensure your happiness. In fact, I've already taken steps to do so. Even before I knew the heartbond would form between us."

"What do you mean?" I shift on his lap as his balls vibrate gently beneath my numb bottom. My pussy isn't numb, however, and I feel every blissful tremor. "What steps have you taken?"

"We've found a habitable planet and we've already altered course. It's called 58-Zallnanis. Sixty-eight percent water. Six large continents that contain lush forests and grassland. It's perfect for humans, but it's also perfect for Darrvasons. My people will be settling on the planet as well. This means the brides we take will be able to visit their families and friends on occasion. You'll live on the same planet as your mother and sister."

Disbelief courses through me, and it takes a full minute for his words to sink in. I almost pinch myself to make sure I'm not dreaming. It sounds too good to be true. Tears blur my vision, and my throat tightens with emotion. The thought of even talking to my mother and sister again is wonderful, but to know I will live on the same planet as them and be able to drop in for a visit? Tornn couldn't have given me a greater gift.

"Thank you," I say, blinking hard as a few tears cascade down my cheeks. My mate is quick to wipe them away, and his expression turns so gentle that it makes me want to weep harder.

"You are welcome, little female." He exhales a long breath as an uncertain look falls over him, then he leans forward and places a lingering kiss to my forehead.

I swoon and swoon.

"I have also ordered the team of Darrvason engineers who were deployed to the *Jansonna* to install video comms in a community room aboard your people's worldship. In a matter of days, you'll be able to speak with your mother, sister, and friends. I'm afraid docking the *Haxxal* to the *Jansonna* to allow visitors isn't an option—given what happened with Paddax and Sheila, it simply isn't safe at this time. But perhaps in six moon cycles, you can enjoy a brief reunion with your family before we settle on whatever continent my people select on Planet 58-Z."

Joy resounds within me, and the tears that slide down my face are borne of happiness. Hope blossoms in my chest. I'd thought my future as a Darrvason bride would be bleak and devoid of warmth and connection. But discovering that my mate had already taken steps to ensure my happiness before the heart-bond started forming between us is the proof I desperately need. The proof that I mean something to him.

Logically, I know things aren't perfect between us. He's kept secrets from me and pushed me away, but haven't I done the same to him? I never told him about Nathan. I've been keeping my own secrets.

I know I must make a full confession soon. Before it's too late. Before anyone gets hurt or worse. I must tell Tornn about the text messages from Nathan and the possible plot against the Darrvason Empire.

It takes me several minutes to find my voice, I'm that choked with emotion, my throat so tight that it's a struggle to breathe. As I shift on Tornn's lap, my pussy quakes with soreness. In the aftermath of our argument and the appearance of his ancestral markings on my arms, he'd pounded me harder than ever before, claiming me with a fierceness that bordered on violence.

"Thank you, Tornn," I finally say as he wipes at my fresh fallen tears. "This means more to me than you'll ever know."

He presses his lips to mine and I melt.

Chapter 30

TORNN

As soon as I stride into the medical bay, Doctor Groaa, the physician who'd recently examined Ellie, ushers me into a private consultation room. I'm still shaking.

In the aftermath of the heartbond that had started forming between me and Ellie, I can't seem to stop trembling.

I'm so ravenous to claim her and pump her full of my seed, that I can barely form a coherent thought. The need to be at her side is overwhelming, and it feels wrong to leave her and possibly miss the formation of another glowing symbol on her arms. When I'd departed my quarters, her left arm was completely covered and the first two markings had already appeared on her right arm.

"I know why you're here," Doctor Groaa says.

"And I know you're in physical pain. Until the heart-bond finishes forming between you and your mate, being away from her side might very well cause you to descend into madness. Please listen to what I have to say, then immediately return to your human bride."

My hands curl into fists and I glare at the male, trying to grasp the meaning of his words. I growl and nod, hoping he'll understand that I want him to continue speaking. If he doesn't hurry up, I might rip him to shreds in a fit of animalistic fury.

"It usually takes several moon cycles for heart-bonds to begin forming between two mated Darrva-sons. I'll admit I'm perplexed by the fact that yours has started forming already, particularly when we always believed it wasn't possible for our people to share such an intense, permanent bond with an alien female. I'm not aware of any other human females experiencing the same symptoms as Ellie, however, I suspect that it's only a matter of time before I learn of another case."

My veins burn and I feel hot all over. I force in a few deep breaths and give a slight nod so the physician understands that I'm listening. I make an urgent gesture with my hands, encouraging him to finish up. If I don't return to Ellie soon, I'm going to burn the whole *fluxxing* ship down.

"I know it's been a while since any male among us has entered a mating bond with a female. Over two decades, in fact. So perhaps you do not recall the mating frenzy that occurs as the ancestral markings appear on the female's arms. But for your own good, and for the safety of all those on the ship, I am pulling rank and ordering you to return to your quarters and remain there until your fever abates."

"My fever?" I blurt out, then realize just how hot I am. I'm sweltering. And my vision keeps blurring.

"Yes. Your bonding fever and your temper will cool once the markings on Ellie's arms finish appearing. It might take a day, or it might take a moon cycle. As I've said, the time frame is different for each couple. Go. Go now."

I don't remember the walk to my abode, but somehow, I'm running down the corridor and the door to my quarters zips open as I rush inside. The scent of my mate hovers in the air, a sweet but pungent aroma that makes me ravenous. I growl as I stalk from room to room, searching for Ellie. I need her. I need her in my arms. I need to bury my cocks inside her and feel her convulse around my lengths as she shatters.

I find her sitting in front of the large viewscreen that overlooks the Darrvason fleet. She turns as I approach, but before she can utter a word, I shove her to the floor on her hands and knees, flip up the skirt of her gown, tear her panties away, and situate myself between her pale thighs. With a hard thrust of my hips, I drive home and immediately start pounding her with my lower shaft.

Her moans and whimpers fill my head, the sweetest *fluxxing* music I've ever heard. Her delicious feminine scent becomes an aphrodisiac to my system, causing me to pound her hard as the sound of flesh slapping flesh resounds off the walls.

I'm not gentle. I'm a beast, a violent space pirate from days of old, and I vaguely wonder if she'll forgive me for my roughness. But no matter how hard I try, I can't be gentle.

To her credit, she moans and gyrates in tune with my rapid thrusts, and her pussy keeps getting wetter. She's soaking for me. And as my vibrating scrotum impacts her clit, I feel just how swollen it's become.

We're facing the viewscreen and the fleet and the stars beyond as I pound her, slamming into her with relentless savagery as I claim and claim and claim. She's *mine* and may the Star Gods help anyone who dares to come between us.

Her insides contract around me, and her first climax ushers in one of my own. I dig my fingers into her hips, admiring the beautiful birthmarks on her back, as I release my seed into her tight depths.

Panting breathlessly, I withdraw my cock and watch with satisfaction as some of my blue seed trickles from her core and runs down her inner thighs. Splaying her bottom cheeks wide with one hand, I scoop up a generous amount of my essence from her thighs with the other, then delve a cum-covered digit into her puckering hole.

She shrieks and jerks as I release a dominant growl, a warning that she better remain still and accept my finger in her ass. I regret that I haven't trained her to accept one of my shafts yet. How I long to surge into her snug little hole and spurt my essence deep inside as she whimpers and moans and the scent of her arousal grows stronger.

Perspiration runs down my temples as I push deeper in her bottom. "One day soon I will pound you with both my shafts. One in your soaking pussy and one in your puckering hole." I growl and align my upper shaft at her center, then give a brutal surge forward as my balls tense and vibrate on her pulsing button.

She quivers and orgasms the instant my scrotum touches her clit, my eager, responsive little female. My heartbonded mate. With my seed-coated finger still submerged in her bottom, I fall into a frenzy of lust as I claim her over and over again, switching from shaft to shaft, repeatedly spurting inside her.

I've never known such fervent, blinding desire, and I vaguely wonder if my ravenous hunger will ever be sated. But maybe it doesn't matter. I could exist in this moment forever, fucking her with vicious strokes as her insides contract around my shafts, her sweet moans and whimpers drifting from her delicate, slender throat.

Chapter 31

ELLIE

EVEN THOUGH TORNN'S ANCESTRAL MARKINGS appeared quickly on my left arm, it takes several days for the remaining symbols to transpire on my right arm. But when the final mark appears, both our fevers begin to cool, and it's like I'm catching my breath for the first time in weeks. But according to my mate, only five days have passed.

As we lay on the bedroom floor holding onto one another—because at some point during our last frenzied joining we'd tumbled off the bed—I become aware of my intense hunger and parched throat. I have faint memories of eating and drinking quickly in between mating sessions at Tornn's insistence, but I don't think either of us has partaken in a proper meal since the ancestral markings unexpectedly began appearing on my arms.

Tornn presses a kiss to my forehead. I sigh and snuggle deeper into his arms, content to stay just like this even if I starve. But when my stomach won't stop growling, he gathers me in his arms and stands up, carrying me into the kitchen. To my surprise, he replicates large portions of hearty vegetable soup, macaroni and cheese, and garlic bread. Human foods.

"Your people have been busy," I say as I accept a bowl of soup. I lean against the counter, too fatigued to walk to the table. But I soon sink to the floor with my legs crossed and devour my soup before Tornn has a chance to pass me a utensil.

He chuckles and joins me on the floor. There's an ease between us that feels natural, and there are times I can sense the heartbond we share. According to Tornn, in time we'll both be able to send emotions and perhaps even thoughts to one another through the bond. I'm not sure how I feel about that, but I realize there's no going back, no way of severing the new connection that's formed between us.

"Tornn," I say, setting the bowl of soup aside, "there's something I must tell you. It's rather important, and I'm afraid you won't like it." I gulp hard as he turns and gives me his full attention.

"What is it?" His eyes narrow with suspicion, and guilt pangs through my insides.

Now that we're *fully* mated—now that I'm wearing his ancestral markings and we share a heartbond—I can't keep Nathan a secret anymore. Oh how I wish I'd trusted Tornn sooner. And I wish Nathan had never put me in this position in the first place. But my allegiance is to my mate, and for the sake of all those I care about on the *Jansonna*, I must ensure the alliance isn't broken. Even if it means Nathan and his accomplices must face justice, though I pray there will somehow be a peaceful resolution to this entire mess.

"Ellie?"

I sigh. "Before I was selected as a Darrvason bride, I was romantically involved with a man on the *Jansonna*. His name is Nathan and we'd planned to get married a few moon cycles from now."

The sudden rage that gleams in Tornn's eyes steals my breath. I expect him to scream at me or growl or grab me roughly. But he doesn't utter a sound or make the slightest move. He simply stares at me as though he wants to murder me.

"I never told you about him because I thought you would be angry, and because I feared you might harm him. Nathan and I never consummated our relationship—you are the one and only male with whom I've copulated—but we were great friends and I-I used to think we were in love."

Tornn growls and grabs my arm, and I gasp when there's a sharp tug on my mind, as though he's trying to peer directly into my thoughts. I sense numerous emotions from my mate, but anger, surprise, and worry are the most predominant. I nearly gasp again when I realize the cause for his worry—he fears I still harbor tenderness for Nathan.

"It's you I want, Tornn, not Nathan," I'm quick to reassure him. I open my eyes and peer into his dark purple depths. Warmth and relief suddenly flow through our bond, but the undercurrent of Tornn's volatile mood remains, and I know without a doubt that he wants to harm my former fiancé. "Look, I-I'm telling you about Nathan right now because I think he's involved in a plot against the Darrvason-human alliance. You know that reading tablet I have? Well, Nathan has been sending me messages on it and—"

Tornn releases a savage roar and tightens his grip on my arm. He leans closer and my stomach flips at the darkness that's gathering in his eyes. *We're mated*, I remind myself. *We share a heartbond. He won't hurt me. He won't.*

I focus on the tether that links our souls, trying to send warmth through it. A wave of submission crashes over me and I also send that emotion through the bond. In response, his grip on my arm loosens, and I sense his control slipping back into place.

Tornn lifts me in his arms and carries me back to the bedroom. He places me on the bed and joins me, urging my thighs apart and situating his lower shaft at my entrance, though he doesn't plunge into my depths. "How did Nathan penetrate our shields to get messages through to you?" He presses lightly against my center, and my hips jerk in response.

"I'm not entirely sure how he did it. But he said he was using an encrypted but fluctuating comm number, so even if your people detected transmissions coming from the *Jansonna*, you wouldn't be able to pinpoint exactly where the messages were coming from on the ship."

Tornn leans down and nips at my ear, his sharp

teeth digging into my flesh. His tongue darts out and he laves at my neck. Shivers rush through me, and I'm very aware that he's not happy with me right now. I'm aware that he might decide to punish me. He presses his shaft harder to my entrance but still doesn't shove inside.

Finally, he draws back and peers down at me, and I sense a surge of power zipping down the bond. I whimper and have a difficult time holding his gaze.

"Tell me everything, sweet human." His face hardens. "I want a full confession."

———

TORNN

As it turns out, Ellie doesn't know any details about the plot against my people. It sounds like little more than a rumor, but it infuriates me that she's known about it for a while but hasn't breathed a word until now. The fact that she's been furtively communicating with another male also infuriates me. How dare she.

Secrets. My little female has been keeping secrets.

I listen as she tearfully describes the text conversations with the human male she'd once intended to marry. Shocks of cold flow down the heartbond, and it takes me a few moments to understand it's her fear that I'm sensing. Her fear of me. She fears my reaction to the news she's sharing.

But she's smart to be afraid. Because I'm currently envisioning myself taking a strap to her bottom, her back, and perhaps even her breasts. I'm thinking about the most painful, humiliating methods of punishment.

When she starts pleading for mercy, my shafts thicken and my balls vibrate faster, the need to conquer her heats my blood and blurs my vision.

"Please understand the position I was in, Tornn. Please don't be angry. If I would've immediately told you about Nathan's texts and the plot, it would've meant his death and the deaths of his accomplices, either by your order or Captain Warren's. While I don't love Nathan anymore—and I'm honestly not sure if love was truly what I once felt for him—I don't want to be responsible for a rash of executions on the worldship."

Thrusting forward, I impale her with one rapid drive, surging deep in her tight pussy. Despite her fear, she's drenched for me, and the scent of her arousal fills my lungs with each breath I take. I remain submerged inside her, unmoving, and lean down to stare her directly in the eyes.

I sense her regret through the bond. It's a flood of desperation that causes my rage to cool somewhat.

"Please, Tornn." She blinks and a few tears slide down her face. Her lips tremble, and her entire body shakes as I remain unmoving inside her, my lower shaft throbbing hard in her pussy, my erect upper cock resting upon her stomach as my balls vibrate against her ass.

"Please what?" I lean down and lick her tears away.

"Please try to understand things from my perspective. Please try to understand that I want the alliance to succeed as much as you do. If at any point, I'd thought there was an imminent threat, I would've said something sooner. I-I just kept hoping that nothing would come of the plot. I'd hoped to change his mind, but then he insulted me and called me some names, and we haven't spoken since."

Rage flares inside me, but it's not Ellie I'm angry with. "What names did he call you?"

I sense her hurt and betrayal through the bond, her surprise over the way Nathan has treated her since she's come to live on the *Haxxal*. And it makes me want to slice the repugnant human man's throat.

"He said I was a traitor and a whore. And he was angry that I wouldn't tell him your name. Whenever he asked who I was mated to, I-I couldn't bring myself to tell him your identity. I felt... protective of you."

Her confession cools my anger further, and I'm no longer envisioning myself tying her up and thrashing her with the strap until my arm grows tired. I cup her face in my hands and experience a resonating warmth in my chest that seems to flow from my heart to hers. Her eyes widen and I know she feels it too.

I gaze upon the markings that cover her arms, and the current of warmth becomes stronger. Not for the first time since the markings appeared, awe fills me. It's a shocking turn of events that Darrvasons and humans can share a true mating bond.

After taking a few deep breaths, I give myself fully to the warmth that's flowing through the tether between our hearts. I sense Ellie's sincerity and her openness, and I don't think she's holding anything back, though the bond is new and I'm still not accustomed to it. I pray she's told me all she knows about Nathan and the plot. I pray she's not intentionally guarding any additional secrets.

The protectiveness she feels for me—the reason she withheld my name from her former fiancé—well, it makes my *fluxxing* throat burn. I doubt there's any way the human male or his comrades could cause me harm, but her desire to protect me is another testament that her loyalties lie with me. That her heart belongs to me, and likewise mine belongs to her.

"Sweet human, I believe you, and I know just how sorry you are for keeping these secrets from me." I press a lingering kiss to her forehead, and she shudders as relief floods the bond. "My cousin, Officer Brute, is currently stationed on the *Jansonna*. I sent him to watch over your uncle and make sure he doesn't harm any of the Darrvason brides' families. I will ask him and the engineers who are currently making repairs on the worldship to quietly investigate Nathan and his comrades. We'll do that before we alert Captain Warren, as I don't want him or his command team to interfere with our investigation."

"Thank you, Tornn." A worried look enters her eyes, and though I can't yet read her thoughts, I know she's wondering if I intend to punish her. I haven't yet decided whether to take a whip to her, kiss her senseless and hold her in my arms, or claim her until she's too sore to walk for days. Perhaps all three. Judging by the immense shame I sense through the bond, I suspect she might need help alleviating her guilt.

"Paddax was released from the medical bay this morning," I inform her, "and Sheila has already been returned to his custody. He has promised to contact me the instant he extracts a confession from her. It's possible Nathan and his group had something to do with her attack on Paddax. If this is the case, then she might be able to tell us more about the group and any other plans they might have."

She pales a bit, and a quick breath escapes her. "I hope Paddax is able to learn something useful, and I hope Sheila confesses before he starts to torture her."

"He won't torture her. She's his mate, and he still intends to claim her. The worst he'll likely do to her is—"

"Whip her? Spank her?" Ellie shivers and her insides tighten around my cock. "What if she refuses to confess? What if he loses control and really hurts her?"

"That won't happen."

"I would like to speak with her. Please. Let me talk to her before he takes a strap to her. Maybe I can convince her to—"

"*No.*"

"No?" A spark of anger lights in her eyes, and frustration sweeps down the bond.

I grasp her hips, withdraw slightly from her center,

then slam back inside, so hard she winces and cries out.

"No," I repeat. "Sheila is Paddax's mate. Whether he's fully claimed her yet or not, I won't interfere in their mating union. Not only is he capable of questioning her, but it's his right to do so. Besides, she was returned to him some time ago. If he was going to take a strap to her, he's probably done so already. You would be too late." I give her another thrust, though this one is gentler.

Her frustration gives way to understanding, and she finally nods as the anger fades from her eyes. Her worry about Sheila is admirable, as is her desire to help uncover any impending threats to the alliance, but I cannot usurp Paddax's authority to question his mate.

"I never told Nathan about Paddax and Sheila and the hyrospray," she says. "Something held me back from volunteering the information. I guess I didn't want him pressing me for news about the happenings on the *Haxxal*. Somehow, I knew from the very start that I couldn't quite trust him. I was also waiting to see if he would ask me whether Darrvasons were getting sick on the *Haxxal*, but he never did."

I'm still holding Ellie's hips in a firm grip as I slowly plunge in and out of her tightness. Each time I drive forward, her center lurches against me and she releases a tiny whimper. I know she's probably sore from five days of nonstop mating, but I need to be inside her now.

I need to feel her sweet surrender while reminding

her that she will always belong to me, that she will always be subject to my authority.

"Have you told me everything?" I ask. "Are you keeping any other secrets from me, little female?"

Her eyes widen, and apprehension trickles down the bond. "I'm pretty sure I told you everything." She pauses for a moment, a look of contemplation falling over her. "Yes, I did. I'm not keeping any more secrets from you, Tornn, I swear."

I increase the pace of my thrusts. "I sense your honesty through the bond, sweet human." I give her a regretful look. "If only you'd been honest with me from the start." Still driving into her, I lean down and delve a hand into her hair, tugging hard enough to bring fresh tears to her eyes.

"*Please*. Please have mercy, Tornn. I-I am sorry."

I fuck her faster, and her thighs fall wider apart as she accepts the deep, rapid strokes. "Keep begging, sweet human. You know I like it when you beg."

Chapter 32

ELLIE

I'M KNEELING ON THE BEDROOM FLOOR, WATCHING AND listening as Tornn communicates with Officer Brute. With his wrist comm lifted to his mouth as he paces the room, he speaks in rapid-fire Darrvason. Every few seconds, he pauses and Officer Brute says something in return.

My eyes go to the strap that rests on the bed. Tornn placed it there several minutes ago, and my stomach clenches as I imagine the reckoning to come. He hasn't outright told me I would be punished for withholding vital information from him, but I know it's coming, and I know it's going to hurt.

Just after he'd announced that he was about to call Officer Brute, he'd ordered me to kneel on the floor. Then he'd taken the strap out of a nearby drawer and placed the implement on the bed.

How many lashes will he give me? More than five?

As I remain kneeling on the floor, his essence continually leaks out of me and coats my inner thighs, a reminder of his ownership over me. A reminder that I'm his to do with as he pleases.

But I feel awful that I kept Nathan and his stupid texts a secret. With the heartbond in place, I can sense the affection that Tornn harbors for me. I can sense that he truly cares about me and I'm more to him than a broodmare. Now that I'm aware of his true feelings, I wish I would've trusted him sooner.

I hope it's not too late. I hope Nathan and his accomplices can be stopped. And if they get into trouble with the Darrvasons or *Jansonna's* command team, then it's a fate they brought upon themselves. I cannot in good conscience stand by while they threaten the alliance and put innocents on the world-ship in danger.

Still speaking to Brute, Tornn comes to loom over me. He got dressed after our last rough mating session, during which he interrogated me as he fucked me, but I'm still completely naked. Words he spoke to me two weeks ago flit through my mind, and my nervousness increases.

When you've committed an offense and I must punish you, you'll be entirely naked when I do so.

He'd said that while he was undressing me. As he was preparing to spread me wide and search my orifices for contraband. Another flush steals over me.

Tornn crouches down, meets my eyes, and reaches

for one of my nipples. As he continues speaking to Brute, he pinches my hardened peak until I whimper. I almost try to pull back, but I know if I resist him, I'll pay for my disobedience later.

He releases my nipple, only to immediately swat the soft underside of my breast, his flattened fingers landing with a quick, brutal sting. Before I can react, he smacks my other breast. I gasp and resist the urge to rub the sting out of my punished flesh.

He rises to his feet, says one last thing into his wrist comm, then drops his hand to his side, the conversation with Brute apparently over. My pulse races as Tornn sets his full attention on me, his dark purple eyes glittering, an aura of power surrounding him.

"Officer Brute is a skilled spymaster. He's also very good at interrogating our enemies. If a quiet investigation doesn't yield any results, he will personally question Nathan and force a full confession from the male. Whatever the traitorous humans are planning, they will fail."

A chill hastens down my spine, but I remind myself that Nathan brought this upon himself. He could've kept his nose down and done his job and settled on planet 58-Zallnanis with the rest of the worldship. By betraying the Darrvasons and Captain Warren, he's basically sealed his own death warrant.

Tornn turns to the bed and picks up the strap. My stomach bottoms out and it's on the tip of my tongue to start begging. But my mouth goes dry, and I can't summon the words. Tremors ripple through my body and it's all I can do to hold position, kneeling with my hands placed on my thighs.

I lower my head as a wave of remorse hits me, unable to hold Tornn's gaze for a second longer. My hair falls in front of my face, obscuring my vision, and goosebumps prickle my arms. And though I know the strap will hurt, warm pulses surge to my center and my breaths come shallow and fast.

I'm aching for my mate to claim me again.

I'm aching for his touch.

He crouches in front of me again and tips my chin up, forcing my eyes to his. A tear rolls down my cheek, and he leans forward to lick it away as a pleased growl rumbles from his throat.

"Unruly female," he says, though his voice is warm. He leans back to meet my gaze. "How many? How many lashes do you need?"

"What?" Confusion flits through me, but then I sense it—I sense his forgiveness through the bond. His understanding. And I suddenly realize that he wants to help absolve me of the guilt that's twisting my insides.

"How many lashes do you need, Ellie?" He tightens his grip on my chin. "Five? Ten? Even more?"

"Ten," I say through a sob. "Ten."

There's a long silence as he studies me and watches the tears sliding down my face. "Ten it is." A look of resolve hardens his expression. "I won't be gentle with you, Ellie. It's going to hurt."

"I know," I gasp out, shuddering with a mix of trepidation and relief. I hate feeling guilty, and I hate that I disappointed him. He's my mate and I withheld information from him that might prove dangerous. His forgiveness means everything, but I'm relieved that he's going to give me what I need, just as he promised he always would.

He caresses my cheek, wiping at my tears. Then he reaches between my thighs and strokes a finger through my slit. I whimper as he grazes my swollen nubbin, and my knees ache when I jolt forward, my center undulating against his touch.

As he continues rubbing a finger through my soaking wet pussy lips, occasionally stroking my clit, he leans close and says, "Be an obedient little female and assume the proper position for punishment." He nods toward the bed, and I know what I must do.

He helps me to my feet, and I wish I could fall into his arms and let him hold me. But the shame of keeping this huge secret for over two freaking weeks has been eating me alive, and now that all has been revealed, I find myself craving the release of guilt. Craving punishment.

Tornn gives me an encouraging look and gently tucks my hair behind my ears. I suck in a shaky breath, turn, and walk to the bed. Then I bend over the mattress, keeping my bottom lifted high and my legs spread wide.

His footsteps sound behind me, and I feel the warmth of his body before he even touches me. He caresses my ass with one hand, moving from cheek to cheek. Leaning over me, his hot exhales drift along my neck. His hard bulge presses against my bottom, and affection cascades through the bond, a rush of warmth and light. But I also sense his steadfast resolve to administer a fitting punishment.

"I'm going to make it fast and hard, sweet human." He steps back and brings the strap down with a whistling crack.

The pain. Holy fucking shit, *the pain.*

Ten. I'd asked for ten. What the hell was I thinking?

But I can't find my voice to plead for leniency. All I can do is gasp and scream through the searing blows. I lose count as the strap comes down again and again. Rapid whooshes followed by lashes of fire that make my nerve endings scream in agony.

Then all at once it stops, and I'm in Tornn's arms. He sinks to the floor and leans against the bed, holding me close as he wipes at my tears and murmurs softly to me in Darrvason.

Affection continues flowing through the bond, and I cuddle deeper into his embrace, soaking up the comfort and warmth he's offering me. He kisses the top of my head and I melt.

As I lace my arms around his waist, I peer at the glowing markings on his chest and feel the corresponding markings on my arms tingle in response. Another surge of forgiveness and understanding reaches me through the bond, as though Tornn wants to remind me that my sins have been absolved. A sense of peace descends, and I marvel at the strength of the heartbond.

"My sweet human," Tornn murmurs in a voice filled with reverence as he strokes a hand through my long locks. *"My loyal mate."*

Loyal mate.

His meaning sinks deep, and I hug him tighter.

Chapter 33

TORNN

It's the middle of the night when the doorbell to my quarters reverberates. Ellie stirs beside me, blinking her pretty blue eyes open, and gives me a worried look.

"Who could that be?" She winces as she turns over and her welted bottom hits the covers.

"Go back to sleep, sweet human." I kiss her forehead. "I'll return as soon as I can." I slide out of bed and hurriedly dress.

When I open the door, I find Officer Paddax pacing the corridor. He looks up and freezes in his tracks when he spots me.

"She confessed everything," he says. A vein in his temple pulses, and his hands flex at his sides. Agitation ripples off him, and I sense he's eager to return to his mate's side.

I exit my quarters, allowing the door to zip shut behind me. "Walk with me." At this hour, most corridors in the *Haxxal* are empty, though we stick to the royal corridors for added privacy. Though I'm anxious to hear what Paddax has to say, I sense his turmoil, and I wait for him to speak on his own.

"There's a group of traitors aboard the *Jansonna* who call themselves The Saviors," he begins. "Two males from the group threatened Sheila's family and forced her to join their cause. They compelled her to conceal the hypospray and bring it aboard the *Haxxal*. They ordered her to inject her mate with the virus in the hopes that it would spread and wreak havoc on our ship. The Saviors hoped that thousands of us would die and that they would be able to take over the *Haxxal* and repossess the human females."

I growl. "How did The Saviors plan to board the *Haxxal* in the first place? And how did they plan to deal with the remaining thirteen vessels in our fleet?"

"Sheila isn't certain, but she thinks they planned to disable our shields and fly straight into our docking bay. She says the *Jansonna* is equipped with over a dozen small shuttles and believes they planned to use those." He clears his throat and casts a glance up and down the empty corridor. "I don't know for certain how they planned to disable the remaining vessels in our fleet and neither does Sheila, but I have a theory."

"A theory?" I pause in the corridor, and we face one another. "Tell me about this theory of yours."

"They could disrupt the hyperdrive bubble we're traveling in, then quickly create a new hyperdrive bubble that only surrounds the *Haxxal* and the *Jansonna*. Before the remaining vessels could recover from the sharp slide out of hyperdrive, they could disappear, taking our largest, most technologically advanced ship with them."

"That's quite a theory." But then I remember that Nathan was able to penetrate our shields in order to send messages to Ellie. Perhaps the humans are more capable of fighting us than we would've ever imagined.

Paddax frowns. "I hope I'm wrong, of course, but as I considered the many methods the humans might use to take over our ship, it seemed like the most logical one. They didn't want to spread the plague just to kill us. They want our ship and its technology so they can find a habitable planet on their own and keep all their females. They wouldn't settle on planet 58-Z out of fear that we would come looking for them, but with the resources aboard the *Haxxal*, they could survive for decades longer in open space."

"You have a sharp but creative mind, Officer Paddax," I say, meaning it. "Perhaps the next time Emperor Radakk has an opening for an advisor, I will offer him your name."

Paddax gives me a deep nod. "It would be my honor to serve the Darrvason Empire in such a way." He glances over his shoulder in the direction of his quarters. "I believe I've told you all I know, Admiral Tornn. If there is nothing else I can assist you with at this time, I am eager to return to my mate."

"One more thing," I say, raising a hand. "Did

Sheila tell you the names of the two traitors who forced her to join their cause?"

"Actually, yes, she did. One was an engineer named Corey Whittaker, and the other was a security officer named Nathan Gonlaz."

———

THE MOMENT BRUTE'S BEARDED FACE APPEARS ON THE screen, I know he's already had some success in the investigation. There's a victorious glint to his dark red eyes.

"Admiral," he says with a nod.

"Officer." I lean closer to the screen. I'm seated at a communication console in the command room, but there's no one nearby to overhear our conversation. "Well?" I ask. "What can you tell me?"

"There are several groups of traitors among the humans who wish to overthrow Captain Warren, though the groups are poorly organized, and they often fight with one another. The male you asked me to investigate—Security Officer Nathan Gonlaz—belongs to a group known as The—"

"The Saviors," I say, cutting him off.

Understanding dawns on his face. "Ah. Officer Paddax must've been reunited with his rebel mate. I trust he extracted a full confession from her?"

I nod and tell him everything I recently learned, including Paddax's theories about how The Saviors planned to kill all the males aboard the *Haxxal* with a virus and steal the large vessel.

"That is a wild, ambitious plan," he says with a wide grin. "Only one problem—we defeated their little virus before it had a chance to destroy a single one of us." He chuckles. "But The Saviors likely have no way of knowing the plan hasn't worked. None of them are on the command team, and even if they were, it's not as though we speak with Captain Warren and his comrades about the happenings on our vessels. If an illness was spreading on any of our ships, we wouldn't complain to the *fluxxing* human captain about it. Humans possess inferior medical knowledge and technology. They wouldn't be able to help us in any way."

I snort and give a derisive shake of my head. "They probably intend to proceed with their plan regardless of this uncertainty. If they manage to disable our shields, they will likely attempt to board the *Haxxal*."

My cousin's eyes glitter with bloodlust, and his nostrils flare as he straightens and his muscles tense. "With your permission, Admiral, I would like to go *hunting*."

I chuckle. "Cousin, I appreciate your enthusiasm, but even if we had definitive proof that The Saviors were planning to try boarding the *Haxxal*, the terms of the alliance dictate that we must turn any and all traitors over to Captain Warren rather than taking justice into our own hands."

Brute narrows his eyes. "You always ruin my fun, Admiral."

I wave a hand at the screen. "Remain on the

Jansonna and continue as you were. If you learn anything new, contact me at once. I must consult with the emperor and his advisors before I make any decisions regarding The Saviors, but I suspect Emperor Radakk will want us to follow the terms of the alliance and turn the traitors over to Captain Warren. But it's my understanding that the worldship captain is quick to execute traitors. Perhaps he'll let you watch, cousin."

"Very well," Brute says with a dramatic sigh as he leans back in his chair. "I will continue to play the spymaster. But you owe me a strong drink when I return." A dark look enters his eyes. "And a bride. If it's not too much trouble, I would like to claim one of the human females from the next batch we receive."

"Your name is already on the list."

After we say our farewells, I schedule an emergency meeting with the emperor and his advisors for the early morning. If I thought the threat from The Saviors was imminent, I would rouse the males from their beds, but I believe we have more than a moon cycle until the rebel group attempts to board the *Haxxal*. According to our scientists, had the virus managed to spread, it would've taken nearly two moon cycles for the majority of our people to become infected.

When I return to my quarters, I find Ellie sound asleep, curled up on her side underneath the covers. I strip off my clothing and join her, spooning her from behind, though I'm careful not to press against her punished ass. Tomorrow, I'll apply numbing salve to her bottom before I depart for the meeting.

I'm still a bit shocked that she asked for ten lashes. Given the circumstances, I would've let her off with a stern scolding, or perhaps a hand spanking, if not for the immense level of guilt I'd detected radiating through the bond.

At first, I'd been furious with her, but the bond had provided me with a better understanding of her motives. She'd been truly sorry, and I'd sensed the desperation that had led her to keep such secrets in the first place. I'd forgiven her long before I'd brought the strap down across her bottom.

As I hold her close, I stroke her hair and breathe in her fragrant scent. I shut my eyes and focus on the heartbond, sending warmth down the everlasting tether. She stirs in her sleep and emits a soft sigh.

"You are precious to me, sweet human," I whisper into her ear. "So very precious."

Chapter 34

ELLIE

A moan escapes my lips when I roll over in bed, and I immediately turn on my side. *Ouch.* I reach back and tenderly prod my sore cheeks, feeling the welts that are causing me so much pain. But before I can toss the covers back and get out of bed, Tornn appears in front of me holding the container of orange salve. His eyes gleam with warmth as he removes the lid and sits next to me.

"Turn onto your stomach, sweet human, and let me tend to you." He begins to work up a thick lather of the salve on his hands.

Though he's my mate and we share a heartbond, I still can't help but flush with shame as I turn onto my stomach. He flips the covers off me and cups my stinging bottom, taking a cheek in each hand.

"Oh!" I gasp and wince more at the sting. But thankfully, as he rubs the salve into my tenderized flesh, the discomfort soon fades. "Thank you, Tornn. That feels much better."

"You're very welcome." He leans down to kiss one of the ancestral markings on my arms, then continues massaging my backside for another minute or two. A lump forms in my throat at the care he's showing me.

Eventually, he lifts me off the bed and sets me on my feet. He gestures toward the closet. "Get dressed. I have an early meeting, and I must leave soon. But there's something I want to show you first."

I hurry to the closet, ignoring the protest of my aching muscles—apparently that five-day sex fest took a lot out of me—and reach for the first Darrvason-style dress I see. I slip into the blue gown without bothering to don panties and a bra. While I have no idea what Tornn wants to show me, I can sense his excitement through the bond.

I dash back to his side, and he smiles and takes my hand, leading me out of the bedroom. We travel past the main sitting area to what was once an empty nook in one of the corners.

A small table now rests in the nook, and there's a large screen mounted on top of it. Beneath the screen I glimpse a flat surface that glows with various symbols.

My heart skips a beat as I realize what I'm looking at—a video comm. He'd promised to have one installed in his quarters, also promising that I would be able to speak with my mother and sister soon.

"Oh, Tornn." I clasp his hand tighter and bring it to my lips, placing a quick kiss to the back of his hand. Through the bond, I sense his surprise over the gesture, quickly followed by a deep satisfaction.

"You only need to press this button," he says, pointing at the very first one on the flat surface, "to reach your mother and sister. I had a video comm installed in their quarters so they wouldn't have to go to a community room every time they wished to speak with you."

My breath catches, and I place another kiss to the back of his hand. "Thank you, Tornn. That was very thoughtful of you. I'm touched. Truly."

"I can feel your gratitude through the bond, sweet human." He helps me into the chair and pats my shoulder. "I must leave now, but please feel free to use the video comm." He kisses my forehead and sends a rush of warmth down the tether.

Before he exits our quarters, I press the first button and watch as the screen illuminates bright blue. It flashes between blue and red for a few seconds until suddenly my mother's face appears. She smiles broadly at me and gestures to someone off screen. Jenny appears beside her, eyes wide, a disbelieving grin tugging at her lips.

"Mom. Jenny." I blink rapidly, overwhelmed by a surge of joy so strong my throat closes up.

"Ellie," my mother says. "Are you all right?" Her eyebrows lift when she notices the ancestral markings that glow on my arms. After the heartbond finished forming, Tornn had taken great delight in ripping all the sleeves off my various gowns, saying he wanted the entire universe to know that I belonged to him at first glance.

"Yes, Mom. I'm fine. I promise."

"Is it true you're mated to the admiral?" Jenny asks. "Admiral Tornn?"

"Yes, I am. How did you know?"

"An overly grumpy Darrvason officer named Brute oversaw the installation of our private video comm," my mother explains. "After being badgered by your sister for a full hour, he finally told us the name of your mate."

"Oh! Officer Brute," I say. "He's Tornn's cousin."

"Really?" Jenny asks, then she shudders. "I certainly hope Tornn is nothing like him. He wouldn't stop glaring and growling. I don't believe I've ever met anyone so disagreeable in my life."

I bite back a smile. I haven't met Brute yet, but I would imagine he's not much different from Tornn. But I don't want my mother and sister to worry about me, so I say, "My mate is treating me well."

"Nathan misses you," Jenny blurts, and my mother immediately shoots her a stern look. "I pass him in the corridors at least once a day, and he always looks like a complete wreck. Disheveled and with dark circles around his eyes."

My stomach twists and it's on the tip of my tongue to tell them to stay away from Nathan, but I don't want to cause them any additional concern, so I press my lips together as I try to think of a neutral response. Thankfully, my mother saves me.

"Nathan is probably tired because he's been taking extra shifts lately," she says. "All the security officers have. Not everyone is happy about the alliance and tensions have been high."

"What's happening?" I ask, scooting to the edge of my seat. "Are you both safe?"

They exchange a look.

"There have been some protests in common areas, a few instances of vandalism, and supposedly someone has been sending death threats to Captain Warren and members of the command team," Jenny says. "But a guard escorts us to and from class each day—and under Captain Warren's orders, if you can believe that."

"That's good to hear. I mean, the part about the guard, not the protests and vandalism and the death threats." I beam inwardly because I have Tornn to thank for ensuring my family's safety. If he hadn't sent Officer Brute over to keep Captain Warren in line, I suspect my mother and sister wouldn't be so well-protected.

"Tell us about your arms," Jenny says with a nod. "Did, um, your mate force you to get those Darrvason tattoos?"

I brush a hand along my upper arm. "Oh, these aren't tattoos at all." I swallow past the dryness in my mouth, unsure why I'm suddenly so nervous about explaining the markings and the heartbond. "They're Darrvason ancestral markings. All Darrvason males are born with them. Uh, not long after Tornn claimed me as his mate, the markings started to appear on my arms and a... a *heartbond* formed between us."

"A heartbond?" my mother and sister say in unison.

"Yes, and..." My voice trails off when the table starts shaking. It's a slight tremor that gradually becomes stronger. "Mom? Jenny? Are you feeling—"

The screen abruptly goes blank and there's a violent jolt that sends me hurling out of my chair. I hit the floor with a thud and roll onto my side. Thankfully, all the furniture in Tornn's quarters is secured to the floors and walls, so nothing goes flying. Even the paintings and sculptures that adorn the walls remain in place.

I scramble to my feet and rush to the viewscreen. My mouth drops open on a soundless cry when a beam of red shoots from the *Jansonna* and strikes the *Haxxal*. I place a hand on the viewscreen's ledge, bracing myself against the impact.

The stars aren't streaking by in a blur of light, which means the vessels are no longer in a shared hyperdrive bubble. I'm not sure what that means, but an icy chill spreads through me when a dozen shuttles zip away from the *Jansonna*, heading in the direction of the *Haxxal*. Oh shit. Oh fuck.

I rush toward the entryway and attempt to leave Tornn's quarters, desperate to find him and ask him what's going on. But the stupid door won't budge. I bang on the door in hopes of someone hearing me, but there's another blast that sends me to the floor. I get to my feet and move back to the viewscreen. The chill inside me spreads. Why aren't any of the Darrvason vessels returning fire?

A groan shudders through the *Haxxal* and the lights go out. Panic seizes me—I don't like the dark—but seconds later, several dim orbs lining the walls come to life, illuminating Tornn's quarters. Emergency lights. Thank goodness.

I attempt to get the video comm working again, but the screen remains blank. With a frustrated growl, I rush to my tablet and start typing a message to Nathan. Maybe if shit's finally going down, he won't be vague about the details anymore. If he can tell me anything useful, perhaps I can pass the information to Tornn.

Somehow, the Darrvason ships have been disabled. I glance at the viewscreen again. The outer lights lining the alien vessels are all dim, making me suspect all the ships are experiencing power failure. Weapons systems and shields are likely down as well. Otherwise, the shuttles from the *Jansonna* would've surely been shot down.

Speaking of the shuttles, where the fuck did they go? Did they actually board the *Haxxal*? Maybe.

Nathan's frequent but vague promises that we would be reunited make my blood run cold. My hands tremble and a sense of helplessness surrounds me.

I'm trapped in Tornn's quarters. Locked inside and I can't fucking leave. I have no way of finding out what's happening, no way of helping. What if there are wounded in the corridors?

My ire rises that Tornn hasn't yet fixed the controls

on the door to allow me to come and go as I please. I'm wearing his ancestral markings, and from what I understand, it's the ultimate protection against rogue, unmated males. Far better than his scent alone.

Images flash in my mind, followed by a surge of emotion. Tornn. The images and feelings are coming from him. I'm experiencing them through the bond. I see flashes of blaster fire, fists swinging, blood spurting. I hear screams. Human screams. And loud, echoing roars that I instinctively know are Darrvason battle cries.

Worry is Tornn's predominant emotion, closely followed by rage. He's worried for me, his only thought of returning to my side as quickly as possible. But there are dozens of armor-clad humans blocking his path in a narrow corridor.

A metallic screeching followed by rapid footsteps sound behind me, and I spin around in confusion, not understanding how Tornn could've reached me so fast.

Cold terror permeates down to my bones and for a long moment, I can't quite comprehend the sight that's greeting me.

It's Nathan. Somehow, he forced the door open— it hangs partially open at an angle. He's dressed in a thickly padded protective suit. Armor. He's also holding a blaster, and there are more blasters and even some knives affixed to his belt. In his other hand, he's grasping a small black device that keeps flashing green. He glances from the device to my tablet, which I'd left in its usual place near the sofa.

My stomach sinks. He used my tablet to fucking track me.

"Hello, Ellie. I've come to take you *home*."

Chapter 35

TORNN

"Shields are back, Admiral!" Captain Varll's voice blares through my wrist comm. "Power has been restored to the upper decks. Still working on the lower decks. Captain Warren keeps hailing us. Shall we fire upon the *Jansonna*?"

"Graze their starboard with a warning shot. Then hail Captain Warren and order him to surrender control of the *Jansonna* to Officer Brute. If he resists, fire a missile at their weapons system and make it a direct hit."

"Understood, Admiral."

I bark more orders into my wrist comm and to the security officers who are flanking me as I hurry down the royal corridors, anxious to reach Ellie.

"Only one of the human males who boarded the *Haxxal* is still missing," Officer Paddax says with a glance at his wrist comm. "But we have security teams sweeping every room and corridor on the ship. Wherever he is, we'll find him soon and he'll join his comrades in death."

"How did the humans disable our shields and power systems at the same *fluxxing* time?" I shout as I reach the corridor that leads to my quarters. I know I'm needed on the bridge, but I must make sure Ellie is all right. The coldness of her fear keeps hitting me through the bond, and I long to take her in my arms and comfort her.

"An initial report from engineering claims they remotely hacked our systems using Xorrshanan technology. Something they must've acquired at an outpost. They also attempted to push our other vessels out of the shared hyperdrive bubble, as I suspected they might, but it didn't work. All fifteen ships left the bubble at once, though the humans were then quick to use the Xorrshanan technology to temporarily disable every ship in our fleet. A good plan," Officer Paddax says, "if only we were all dying of the plague and couldn't fight back."

"Why do you suppose they attacked us now?" I ask, impressed that Paddax's theories are proving correct. "Had it worked, the virus would've taken two moon cycles to spread through the *Haxxal* and incapacitate our crew. They're over a moon cycle early." They *fluxxing* caught us by surprise.

Officer Paddax squints at his wrist comm. "As you know, they are several millennia behind us in scientific advancements." He snorts and shrugs one shoulder.

"They probably miscalculated the spread of the virus. Fools."

"Take your security team to the bridge," I order Officer Paddax. "I will join you in a moment. There's something I must do first."

To the security officer's credit, he doesn't balk or even lift an eyebrow when he sees me take off in the direction of my quarters. Instead, he draws in a deep breath and starts issuing orders to those under his command, and the entire team veers down a corridor that leads to the bridge.

I rush into my quarters—why the *fluxx* is the door open?—still startled by the powerful surges of fear I sense through the bond.

Just as I pass the entryway, there's a flash of red, and a sharp pain impacts my shoulder. *Fluxx*. Blaster fire. That means…

I growl and barrel toward the human man who's grasping a struggling Ellie by the arm. She punches at his chest and tries to reach his blaster, but he holds it high and attempts to shoot me again. The beam goes wide and hits a painting on the wall to my left.

My rage is a blinding, dark force, the most powerful surge of bloodlust I've ever experienced. *Ellie*. The human scum has his hands on my mate.

Before I can reach them, the male wraps an arm around her, holding her tightly to his chest as he presses the blaster to her temple.

I freeze.

"Stay back!" the human male screams. "Stay the fuck back or I'll shoot her. I swear I'll do it!"

"Let go of me, Nathan. You stupid asshole." Ellie stomps on his foot, and he snarls and presses the blaster more firmly to her head. She goes absolutely still.

Nathan. My bloodlust mounts. So, this is the human male Ellie was supposed to marry. The human male who'd called her a traitor and a whore.

"It's over," I say. "All your comrades are dead, and you'll never make it back to your shuttles in the docking bay."

Nathan's face goes white. "You're lying. There were two hundred of us packed onto the shuttles. Our soldiers can't all be dead."

As I press my hand to a hidden pocket on my pants, feeling the outline of the small but deadly weapon hidden within, I give the human male a broad, menacing smile, making sure to reveal my sharp, pointed teeth. "All dead," I repeat.

"Why aren't you all sick?" Nathan asks in a wavering voice. "Fuck. You were all supposed to be sick or dead."

"The Darrvasons were quick to save Sheila's mate and develop a vaccine against the virus she injected him with," Ellie says. "I tried to warn you. I tried to tell you that the Darrvasons are much more powerful than us and there's no defeating them."

"Shut up!" He gives her a shake, and I take two steps forward as I withdraw the weapon from my pocket. "You were supposed to be my wife! With Captain Warren's niece as my wife, The Saviors planned to install me as the next captain!"

It takes all my self-control not to growl and launch myself at Nathan, but I cannot risk Ellie getting hurt. A blaster shot to the head would likely kill her. Fortunately, my thick, textured skin offers me protection against the human weapon. I need to get myself between her and Nathan. I need to protect my sweet human female.

As I hold Ellie's gaze, I send warmth down the bond. Her eyes glisten with tears and I feel her grasping onto the affection I'm sending her, holding onto the tether as though she's clasping my hand.

Drop down, drop down, drop down.

I try to send the command through the bond, unsure if it'll work.

Drop down, Ellie. Right now.

I clutch the shooting star between my fingers—a tiny but lethal, metallic throwing blade that has a nerve agent embedded within it. But I can't *fluxxing* toss it at Nathan if there's a chance I'll hit Ellie. I'm a good aim but I cannot risk her safety.

Drop down, Ellie. Drop down.

Her eyes widen and her mouth falls open. My spirits lift when I feel her understanding through the bond, and an instant later, she complies with my order. She lifts her feet up and falls down, slipping through Nathan's grasp as he curses and fumbles not to drop his blaster.

It all happens very fast.

I hurl the shooting star at Nathan's neck, and it sinks deep, slicing his flesh and causing him to gurgle blood. The blaster slips from his hand, tumbling to the floor with a clatter. His face turns blue, and his body convulses as he falls back against the viewscreen.

Before Ellie hits the floor, I dive forward and catch her in my arms, shielding her from the fall. I hold her close as I rise to my feet, then carry her to the sofa and place her down as I scan her for injuries. There's a faint splotch of red on her cheek, and my rage ignites anew as I realize Nathan must've slapped her. I growl and peer over my shoulder at his twitching body as he chokes on his own blood while the nerve agent works to paralyze him.

I turn back to Ellie and place a gentle kiss to the red mark on her cheek, wishing I could've taken my time torturing her former fiancé to death. But with Ellie in his clutches, I'd needed to take him out quickly.

Behind us, the revolting male goes silent.

He's finally dead.

I carry Ellie into the bedroom, not wanting her near Nathan's body, never mind that he can't hurt her anymore. I don't know if the sight of a dead body will bother her, but I want him out of her presence. I settle on a chair with my beloved female in my lap. Lifting my wrist comm to my mouth, I send a quick message to Officer Paddax, informing him of the events in my quarters while also requesting a crew to remove the deceased male.

Ellie peers at the blaster wound on my shoulder and I feel her concern through the bond. As well as her guilt. Though she warned me about Nathan and a possible plot against the alliance, she regrets not telling me sooner. But I don't hold her responsible for the events of today, and I try to convey my feelings on the matter through our connection.

As I send her more affection, I say, "It's over and he's dead. His comrades have already been vanquished. They failed. You mustn't blame yourself for their attack on the *Haxxal*."

"I should've told you sooner, Tornn. I'm so sorry."

I cup her face in one hand, and she leans into my touch. "You already confessed, sweet human, and I've already punished you. It's in the past. Besides, you didn't know any details of The Saviors' plan."

"But you're hurt." She tries to get up, but I tighten my hold on her, reluctant to let her go just yet. "You need to get to the medical bay immediately."

"It's only a scratch, and it'll heal on its own before the day is over." While I could venture to the medical bay and allow a physician to run a dermal regenerator over the injury, I know the doctors are busy tending to injured security officers, and I have no wish to bother them over such a minor wound.

Her eyes go wide. "How did you know Nathan was here?" Her voice wobbles, and she blinks rapidly.

"I didn't. But I felt your fear through the bond, and I rushed to your side as quickly as I could." I run a hand through her hair and press a lingering kiss to her forehead. She emits a soft sigh and snuggles deeper into my arms.

"I can't believe he was using me. For all these years, he-he only wanted me because I was the captain's niece. He thought having me on his arm would make his claim to the *throne* more legitimate. But he's been working with The Saviors all these years. He told me everything. He never really cared about me, and I feel like the biggest fool."

"He's the fool, Ellie. Not you." I send comfort down the bond and nuzzle my face in her hair.

"Thank you for saving me, Tornn. If you hadn't come…" Her voice trails off and she shivers.

"I will always come for you, sweet human, though I hope there are no more threats to your life." I kiss her forehead again. "You're mine, my mate, and you are… precious to me."

Her breath catches, and she pulls back to meet my eyes. "You're precious to me, too."

Chapter 36

ELLIE

In the aftermath of The Saviors' attack, tensions remain high between the Darrvasons and humankind for several weeks. There are occasional uprisings on the *Jansonna*—more factions of rebels who want to overthrow my uncle—but at least I know my mother and sister are safe. Tornn's cousin, Officer Brute, will remain on the *Jansonna* for the foreseeable future, and the security officer frequently checks on my family. He also ensures they always have an armed escort when they leave their quarters, sometimes performing the duty himself.

I suspect there's something going on between my sister and Brute, but whenever I ask, she brushes my questions aside or makes a flippant comment about how rude or arrogant he is.

But I'm very aware of her age. She won't turn

nineteen—the age at which Darrvasons believe a female is ready for breeding—until after we reach 58-Zallnanis, but in human culture, she's already considered an adult. Tornn says I needn't worry—he's promised to keep her off the list of brides. But what if Brute loses control and claims her?

Pushing the dark thoughts away, I wrap a towel around myself as I exit the bathtub. I glance at the timepiece on the wall and my heart skips a beat. Tornn is due to return at any moment. He promised to come home early tonight, a few hours before dinner.

I hurriedly dress in the purple gown. It's always been my favorite since it matches his eyes so well. I decide to forgo a bra and panties. Thanks to Tornn's propensity for ripping them off my body, I'm running low on undergarments.

Just as I exit the bedroom, I hear the door zipping open. Warmth fills me, a combination of my own excitement over Tornn's return and the affection he's sending through the heartbond. The connection we share has taken getting used to—it still shocks me sometimes when I hear his voice in my head—but overall, I'm glad for it.

If not for the bond, I doubt he would've been so understanding and forgiving after I made the confession about Nathan. I shudder to think how severely he would've punished me if he'd stumbled upon the messages without context. I also shudder to think how long it would've taken me to earn his trust.

"Hello, sweet human." Tornn opens his arms and I step into his embrace.

As I snuggle deeper into his arms, I feel something hard pressing against me that doesn't quite feel like his erect cocks. Curious, I step away and glance at his center. "What's that?" I gesture at his pocket.

His purple eyes glitter darkly and his nostrils flare. I flush as I realize he's inhaling the scent of my arousal. I can't help it. Just being in his presence and basking in the warmth of his arms is enough to get my hyperdrive running.

He withdraws a long metal box from his pocket and flips open the lid, revealing the contents.

My bottom clenches involuntarily and I take a step back. I think of the naughtiest books on my tablet and vaguely recall the characters in some of them using sex toys, including... butt plugs.

I'm not certain, but I *think* I'm staring at a set of plugs. For my poor innocent butt. The smallest is about the circumference of Tornn's pointer finger, while the largest is nearly as big as his upper cock.

A quiver rushes over my bottom cheeks, and a heated flush sweeps through me. Suddenly, I'm sweltering in the confines of my gown, and I can't seem to catch my breath.

"Um, Tornn?"

"I promised you I would one day claim both your holes at the same time, Ellie, and your training begins tonight." He closes the box and nods toward the bedroom. *Go prepare yourself for me, sweet human. You know I want you naked, and you know the exact position I expect you to assume. Obey me.* He says this last part through the bond, and despite my hesitation, a wave of submission crashes over me.

Whenever he sends me orders through the bond, my body reacts in a visceral manner and it's almost impossible to disobey.

After casting a worried look at the box, I traipse to the bedroom, my trepidation growing with each step. With shaking hands, I remove the gown, wondering why I even bothered getting dressed in the first place. It's a rare event when Tornn doesn't pounce on me within ten minutes of returning to our quarters.

I approach the bed, my hands shaking at my sides, as I imagine what it'll feel like to have a plug inserted in my bottom hole. Warmth quakes between my thighs and my breasts feel heavy, my nipples tightening to sharp peaks. I take a deep breath, then bend over the bed, assuming the position I know he prefers.

Most of the time, he claims me from behind while I'm bent over the bed just like this. Given the extra equipment he's packing in his pants, I suspect it's the most comfortable method of lovemaking for him.

I move my legs wide apart and lift my butt high in the air. A needy whimper drifts from me as I await his arrival. I'm aching for his touch even though I'm certain he's going to push my limits. Even though I'm worried the plug will hurt.

I feel his presence before he speaks, a dominating force that overpowers but also anchors me. I glance over my shoulder, and when our eyes collide, my breath catches and my pulse flutters. God, he's so fucking handsome, his features regal yet ruggedly masculine. He's standing in the doorway, the box of plugs in his hand, a massive bulge tenting his pants.

He speaks to me through the bond.

What an obedient little female you are.

Look at that wet, swollen pussy. I'm going to fuck you there after I shove a plug in your tight asshole, sweet human, and you'll have no choice but to lay there and take the hard pounding I give you.

I flush and turn back around to grip the covers. He sets the box on the bed in my line of vision, and I can't help but watch as he flips the lid back again. But to my shock, he doesn't withdraw the smallest plug. Instead, he goes for the next size up.

"Hey!" I protest. "That's the wrong one! It-it's larger than your finger."

A dark chuckle escapes him, then he clutches my left butt cheek hard, digging his fingers into my flesh until I whimper from the pain. "It's not the wrong one, Ellie. I'm *training* you, and I don't think the smallest plug will provide much of a challenge. It's the same size as my finger and you already do so well with my finger plunging in and out of your ass." He releases my butt only to administer two hard spanks, one to each cheek. "Say another word about it and I'll select an even larger plug. Or maybe I'll forgo the plugs entirely and shove my cock straight into your bottom hole. Maybe that's what you need. A hard punishment fuck in the ass."

"No, please." I whimper as I tense my butt, as though clenching will stop him from drawing my cheeks wide apart. "*Please.* I-I'm sorry." Holding my breath, I pray he doesn't decide to skip the plugs. Both his cocks are so huge, I don't think I could take either one of them. Not yet. Not without it really hurting.

He leans over me, and the hardness of his erections presses against my bottom. His warm breath dances over my ear as he sends a surge of power down the bond, further compelling my surrender. A growl rumbles from his chest and vibrates through my insides, causing the heated pulses between my thighs to come faster. "That's it, sweet human, beg. Beg me for mercy."

TORNN

"*PLEASE PLEASE PLEASE.*" ELLIE WHIMPERS AGAIN AND I sense her nervousness through the bond, and *fluxx* it makes my cocks harder than *Rulliann* steel.

I step back and grasp her bottom, taking a cheek in each hand and pulling her ass wide apart, revealing her shy puckering hole. A groan leaves me as I watch it wink a few times.

So small and tight, but like the rest of my human mate, that hole belongs to me.

It's my right to train her to accept my upper cock in her most private place and that's exactly what I plan to do. No matter how much she begs. *Especially* if she begs.

Keeping her bottom splayed open with one hand, I retrieve a jar of lubrication from the box and scoop a generous amount onto my finger. As her snug hole clenches against my ministrations, I rub the lube into her pucker, preparing her for the intrusion of the plug.

"Please, Tornn."

Fluxx, is she trying to make me lose control? All I can think about is how good her ass will feel gripping my upper shaft.

Though I sense her trepidation through the bond, another emotion comes to me, a spark of mischief that she's trying to conceal. I growl. She's begging so sweetly just because she knows how much I enjoy it.

Naughty human. Are you daring to tease me?

She jolts, clearly hearing my voice in her head.

I continue massaging the lubrication into her pucker, then I grasp the second to smallest plug and gently push the tip inside her ass. She rises on her toes and squeals, though she doesn't attempt to move out of position otherwise.

Keep holding still, sweet human. If you fight me, I'll get the strap.

"Please, no. I'll be good. I promise. Please not the strap." She shudders and I push even deeper, watching as her hole stretches around the plug.

Once the plug is fully seated in her bottom, I release her cheeks and step back to free my cocks from my pants. Desire pummels me and I feel nearly as feverish as I did during the mating frenzy as we became heartbonded.

"How does it feel, Ellie?" I ask as I stroke my lower

shaft, my gaze on the base of the plug that's visible between her cheeks. My eyes drift to her swollen pink folds and I groan. The scent of her arousal is making me ravenous.

"It feels… too big. Please, Tornn. Please take it out."

Again, that spark of mischief floats down the bond, and I know without a doubt that she can handle the plug. I sense her discomfort, but as I tug on the bond, sending her warmth and pulling her heart closer to mine, I don't sense any pain.

I move closer and run a hand down her back, observing as goosebumps rise on her arms. My heart swells with affection as I gaze upon the ancestral markings she wears. The proof of our unbreakable bond. The proof that she will belong to me forever.

Fisting my lower cock, I align it with her slick pussy, then shove the bulbous head inside. She moans and writhes against the sudden fullness. I grasp her hips, emit a thunderous growl, and give a violent thrust forward, fully sheathing my thick member in her sopping wet channel.

"Perhaps after a moon cycle of training," I say, tapping at the plug, "you'll be ready to take both my cocks inside you."

Adjusting my hold on her hips, I set a rapid pace of claiming her, surging into her depths over and over as my vibrating scrotum slams into her clit. I fuck her hard and without mercy, ignoring her whimpering pleas.

"Settle down, human," I say in a stern voice. "You

belong to me, and I will fuck you whenever I want, as hard and long as I want, and you will *fluxxing* take every stroke until I spurt my seed inside you." I growl. "Be obedient and let me claim what's *mine*."

Her insides suddenly clamp down and pulse around my cock. She cries out, clumsily undulating her center as she attempts to meet my rapid thrusts. A savage roar leaves me and I push deeper and erupt inside her, my own climax stealing my breath and making my vision blur. I gasp and growl and revel in the feel of her tightness.

When I finally withdraw from her pussy, my blue seed trickles down her inner thighs. I grip her bottom cheeks, pulling them wide apart to better glimpse the plug, which only causes more of my essence to spill out of her pussy. Her embarrassment reaches me through the bond and makes my unspent shaft pulse with excitement.

I position my upper cock at her cum-drenched entrance and surge home, driving in and out of her, a bit more slowly this time, as I allow my vibrating balls to rub against her engorged button.

Pressing so very deep, I remain fully submerged inside her and wait for the quaking release to hit her. The moment her pussy walls start contracting around my length, I resume pummeling her with my shaft. Finally, I erupt in her for a second time, filling her with more of my seed.

She whimpers and moans as I pull out of her center, her entire body quivering in the aftermath of her releases. The delectable scent of her arousal remains thick in the air, and *fluxx* I can't get enough of it.

Kneeling behind her, I bury my face in her pussy, licking her clit and tasting the mix of her pungent excitement with the sweetness of my seed. She shatters almost instantly, but I don't stop.

"*Please please please*, Tornn. Too much. It's too much. I can't, I can't…"

Come for me again, sweet human. Do as you're told.

She jolts her slick center against my roving tongue and cries out, lost in the throes of another orgasm. My obedient little female.

I rise to my feet, wipe my mouth on my arm, and gently withdraw the plug from her ass. She remains in place, panting breathlessly, my essence trickling down her inner thighs to pool on the floor at her feet. A mess for the android to clean up later.

I turn her over and lift her in my arms, carrying her to the bathroom. Her soreness and fatigue reach me through the bond, but so does her immense satisfaction, and she peers up at me with a tiny smile tugging at her lips.

"You did well, sweet human," I say in a praising tone.

Once the tub is filled with soapy water, I sink down in the bath with Ellie still in my arms. She leans her head against my chest with a contented sigh. She fits in my arms so perfectly that I believe the Star Gods must've fashioned her just for me.

I brush her hair behind her ears and kiss her forehead.

She laces her arms around my waist and buries her face deeper in my chest, her soft exhales tickling my flesh. I comb my fingers through her hair and breathe deep of her scent, and we take turns sending one another warmth through the bond.

"Do you think we're in love?" she asks, pulling back to meet my eyes. "Do you think we're truly in love, or do you think it's the heartbond forcing it?"

I take a moment to ponder her question. "Even before the heartbond formed, sweet human, you were precious to me."

She blinks fast as tears fill her eyes, and I sense her relief over my response. "You were precious to me, too, Tornn. Before the bond. I tried to resist it, but I felt an overwhelming warmth for you before the first ancestral marking appeared on my arm." She traces the markings on my chest, and I send her my love.

Epilogue

ELLIE

TONIGHT'S THE NIGHT. A FULL MOON CYCLE HAS passed since Tornn started training me to accept the plugs in my ass, and I know he intends to give me a double pounding with his dual shafts tonight.

Before he left for his final shift on the bridge, I caught a hint of dark pleasure through the bond and saw a clear image of his lascivious intentions. A mental picture so naughty it made me blush and nearly tempted me into touching myself in his absence.

For the last week, I've managed to take the largest plug in my ass. But I can't help but feel nervous because *holy hell his shafts are both huge.*

I assume he'll shove into me from behind, and this brings me a tiny measure of comfort. Because it means his upper cock (which is slightly smaller than his lower cock) will probably be the one he shoves in my bottom hole.

I pace in front of the viewscreen as I await his return, occasionally glancing at the Darrvason fleet and the *Jansonna*. Three more months. Only three months until we reach planet 58-Z.

Longing fills me as I imagine stepping onto real land with Tornn at my side. I suspect I'll likely drop onto my hands and knees and kiss the ground.

Not only am I looking forward to setting foot on a planet for the first time, but I'm anxious for a reunion with my mother and sister. I'd hoped that perhaps they could visit the *Haxxal*, but tensions are still high and the emperor's advisors believe it's too dangerous to dock the *Haxxal* to the *Jansonna*. And all the world-ship's shuttles are still in the *Haxxal's* docking bay. The Darrvasons won't return the shuttles until humankind is settled on 58-Z, the final two thousand women handed over, the terms of the alliance honored.

Speaking of human women, repairs were finally completed on the *Jansonna*, which means the group of one hundred will be arriving in a matter of days, though not all of them will be claimed by Darrvason males on the *Haxxal*. This group will be split amongst the various ships in the fleet, each vessel sending a shuttle to the *Jansonna* to retrieve the women. From what I understand, security will be tight, and the women won't be permitted to bring any possessions.

I can't help but wonder if any of my friends will be in the new group. It's a conflicting thought. On the one hand, I would love to be reunited with people I know and care about. On the other hand, I know many of the Darrvason males are more possessive than Tornn and I can't in good conscience wish that sort of life upon my friends or acquaintances.

A sigh escapes me as I think about the women from our original group of thirty. The very first payment given to the Darrvasons. It's been three months since we were all selected by a Darrvason male in the *Haxxal's* docking bay, yet I've only run into about ten of those women in the corridors so far. The others haven't been permitted free roam of the *Haxxal* by their mates yet, a thought that saddens me, though I hope in time their mates will finally let them out.

Thalia. I haven't seen her yet, and I'm starting to worry. Why won't the emperor allow her any freedom? He won't even walk with her in the corridors. And while Tornn occasionally visits the emperor's quarters for private meetings, he's yet to catch a glimpse of Thalia during his visits.

But Tornn repeatedly assures me that she's alive and well, insisting that Emperor Radakk is too level-headed to harm his female. I hope he's right. I hope she's okay.

A noise in the entryway catches my attention, and I turn as Tornn strides toward me, his strong presence filling the room. I push aside all thoughts of 58-Z and the alliance and the other Darrvason brides as he comes closer.

"Hello, sweet human." His deep voice reverberates through me, causing my pussy to clench.

"Hello, Tornn." I swallow hard and suddenly feel

like a virgin all over again. As though he senses this particular thought (and given the heartbond, it's possible he does), a predatory smile spreads over his face.

"I could smell your arousal from the entryway, Ellie." Suspicion gleams in his purple eyes. "Were you touching yourself?"

Shame courses through me at the very notion, and I give a quick shake of my head. "No, Tornn. I wasn't. I swear." Though I've been off the hormone suppression shots for months now and away from the sexually repressive atmosphere of the *Jansonna*, I still can't help but experience shame over the idea of touching myself. In fact, I've only done so twice since becoming Tornn's mate. My bottom cheeks clench as I recall the whipping I'd received after the first instance of self-pleasure, when I'd planned to conceal my actions from him.

My mate's dark gaze roams over my body, and when I notice the huge bulge tenting his pants, the pulses between my thighs become more intense. He releases a low, steady growl and begins removing his clothing.

Remove your gown this instant or I'll tear it off.

I scramble to obey the order he issues through the bond, pulling the dress over my head and tossing it toward the sofa. I stand before him completely naked, wondering if he plans to claim me in front of the viewscreen or if he'll carry me to the bedroom.

He circles me as I stand in place awaiting his next command. Tremors besiege me as my nervousness grows, and I feel a phantom intrusion in my ass even though he hasn't laid a finger on me yet. Even though he hasn't bent me over and shoved a shaft into my tight bottom hole.

He pauses in front of me and reaches between my thighs, drawing a digit through my gathering moisture. I whimper and my center jerks forward. He spreads wetness over my clit then gives it a sharp pinch that brings tears to my eyes. But just as quickly, he releases my nubbin and steps back.

His dual appendages are rock hard and sticking straight out. Drops of his blue essence cling to both tips. He grasps his lower shaft, fisting it in one hand. Then he steps forward, grasps my arm, and leads me behind the sofa. When he gives me a slight push toward the piece of furniture, a vision of me bent over the back of it flits through my mind. I rush to comply and place my hands on the cushions. I flush when he grasps my bottom cheeks and draws them wide apart, further exposing my pussy and revealing my pucker as well.

"Ellie, do you have any idea how long and hard I'm going to fuck you?" he asks in a rumbling tone.

I whimper as tension coils in my lower belly and the warm quaking pulses make my clit throb and throb. I'm a little afraid, but I'm also aching and desperate to be filled up with both my mate's shafts.

"Please, Tornn."

"That's it, sweet human. *Beg me*. Beg me to fuck you with both my cocks." He lines his lower shaft up with my pussy, then I feel his upper cock pressing against my asshole. He reaches behind a pillow on the sofa and withdraws a jar of lubrication, and my pulse accelerates as I realize he must've planned this well in advance.

"*Please*. Oh!"

His fingers are suddenly prodding my ass as he massages a copious amount of lube into my pucker. When I once more feel the pressure of his upper shaft on my bottom hole, I plant my hands more firmly on the cushions and brace myself for the first hard thrust.

He's not gentle. One moment he's applying pressure to both my holes, then suddenly he's inside me, shoving deep into my pussy and ass at the same time. I gasp and the room spins, and as he keeps his vibrating balls pressed directly upon my clit, a wave of bliss crashes over me.

"Good little female. Come on my cocks. That's it."

His words send an erotic thrill through me as I gasp for breath. I'm shaking with the pleasure, the remnants of my release still pulsing through my center.

Tornn growls and starts withdrawing his shafts from my holes, only to immediately slam back inside. *Oh my God. Oh my fuck.*

I can't think, I can't breathe, I can't do anything but remain bent over the sofa as he pounds me hard.

His immense satisfaction reaches me, and I send him a plea to be quick. I hear a mocking chuckle in my head as he tightens his hold on my hips. His huge vibrating scrotum impacts my bundle of nerves with each rapid plunge into my holes. Another orgasm sweeps over me, and my pussy clamps down on his lower shaft as I come so hard I go dizzy.

I lose all sense of time as he claims me. The room fills with the echoes of his growls and the steady smacking noise of his balls hitting my swollen clit.

Just when I think the fullness is too much and that I can't endure another second of his rough pounding, he shoves deeper and roars loud, his cocks pulsing inside me as he spurts violently into my depths.

The rest of the evening passes in a daze of comfort and tenderness. He withdraws from me slowly, lifts me in his arms, and carries me into the bathroom. The water is warm and fragrant and relaxing, and his arms are the sweetest refuge.

Drained of all energy, I bask in the care he shows me and the warmth he keeps sending down the bond. I find myself thinking of the future we'll share on 58-Z and how it won't be bleak and as oppressive as I'd once imagined. Tornn is a possessive male and I know he would never let me go under any circumstances, but I also know he'll protect me with his life and always take care of me.

Children. We'll have children together one day. I'm not pregnant yet, but expect it'll happen soon, and I find myself looking forward to motherhood and watching Tornn grow as a father. The sudden mental image of him cradling a small baby in his arms steals my breath, and when a knowing look enters his eyes, I realize he's sharing my vision.

He sends me a few images of his own—the layout of the first Darrvason settlement on 58-Z, a glimpse of the house he plans to build for us, and what I think must be a school. A second later, he shows *me* standing at the front of a classroom, and I smile at the picture as my heart brims with hope. He's showing me a glimpse of our future and the freedoms I'll be granted.

A sense of peace falls over me as he tucks me under the covers later in the evening. He joins me in bed and gathers me close, and I rest my head on his chest and trail my fingers over his ancestral markings. He strokes the matching marks on my arms and keeps pressing kisses to my forehead.

"My precious mate. My sweet, unruly little female."

About Sue Lyndon

USA TODAY BESTSELLING AUTHOR SUE LYNDON writes naughty, heartfelt romance filled with sexy discipline, breathless surrender, and scorching hot passion. Hard alpha males, strict husbands, fierce alien warriors, and stern daddy-doms make her go weak in the knees. She's a #1 Amazon bestseller in multiple categories, including Sci-Fi Romance, Historical Romance, BDSM Erotica, and Fantasy Romance. She also writes vanilla sci-fi romance under the name Sue Mercury—but no matter the genre or pen name, her books always have a swoon-worthy happily ever after.

WWW.SUELYNDON.COM

Get FREE reads when you sign up for Sue's newsletter—and be the first to hear about freebies, sales, and new releases: https://www. suelyndon.com/newsletter-sign-up ****

Printed in Great Britain
by Amazon